THE KINGFISHER TREASURY OF

Christmas
Stories

KINGFISHER
An imprint of Kingfisher Publications Plc
New Penderel House, 283-288 High Holborn
London WC1V 7HZ
www.kingfisherpub.com

First published by Kingfisher 1994
This edition published by Kingfisher 2005
2 4 6 8 10 9 7 5 3 1

A CIP catalogue record for this book is available from the British Library

ISBN-13: 978 0 7534 1159 9
ISBN-10: 0 7534 1159 8

Printed in India
1TR/0705/THOM/FR(MA)/115INDWF/F

THE KINGFISHER TREASURY OF

Christmas
Stories

CHOSEN BY SIAN HARDY

ILLUSTRATED BY KATE ALDOUS

KINGFISHER

CONTENTS

Acknowledgements

For permission to reproduce copyright material acknowledgement and thanks are due to the following:

A M Heath & Co Ltd for "The Silver Cup" copyright © Joan Aiken 1990; Victor Gollancz and Alfred A. Knopf, Inc. for "The Box" from *More Stories Julian Tells* copyright © Ann Cameron 1986; Hamish Hamilton Ltd and William Morrow & Co, Inc. for "Ramona and the Three Wise Persons" from *Ramona and her Father* copyright © Beverley Cleary 1975; the publisher for "The Christmas Whale" by Roger Duvoisin copyright © Alfred A. Knopf, 1945, renewed by Roger Duvoisin 1973; William Heinemann Ltd and William Morrow & Co Inc. for "Wake Up, Bear . . . It's Christmas" copyright © Stephen Gammell; the author for "Gifts" copyright © Adèle Geras 1990; The Bodley Head for "Christmas Through a Knothole" from *Merry Christmas From Betsy* copyright © Katherine Gibson 1963; William Morrow & Co, Inc. for "A Present for Santa Claus" from *A Christmas Acorn* copyright © Carolyn Haywood 1970; André Deutsch Children's Books for "Early on Christmas Morning" from *The Rifle House Friends* copyright © Lois Lamplugh 1965; The Bodley Head for "The Story of the Christmas Rose" from *To Read and Tell* copyright © Norah Montgomerie 1962; the author for "Room for a Little One" copyright © Maggie Pearson; Hutchinson for "The Mice and the Christmas Tree" from *Little Old Mrs Pepperpot* copyright © Alf Prøysen; William Morrow & Co, Inc. for "The Christmas Roast" copyright © Margaret Rettich, and Faber and Faber Ltd for "The Fairy Ship" from *John Barleycorn* copyright © Alison Uttley.

"Baboushka", "Brer Rabbit's Christmas" and "A Very Big Cat" retold by Nora Clarke, and "The Little Fir Tree" retold by Alison Carter copyright © Grisewood & Dempsey Ltd 1985.

WAKE UP, BEAR... IT'S CHRISTMAS!

Stephen Gammell

As the last few leaves of autumn fell, Bear was padding down his walking trail. He was going home for his winter's sleep. But he wasn't going to be sleeping all winter.

"That's right," he said, as he reached his door. "I've missed it now for seven years, and seems I've heard it said that it's a happy, joyful time, but always I'm in bed. Well, this year things are different. I've decided what to do. I'm getting up for Christmas, instead of sleeping through!"

After setting his clock and fixing his bed, Bear blew out the candle. Feeling happy but tired, he snuggled down under his blanket.

"Well," he yawned, "when I wake up I wonder what I'll see. Anyway, I hope it's fun when Christmas comes to . . .'

He fell asleep.

7

The weeks went by. The forest was still and silent. The only sound was the wind as it blew softly during the day, and harder at night.

The snow started to fall late one afternoon. It fell gently at first, then became heavier. Soon, snow covered nearly everything in the forest. It almost came up to Bear's window.

Bear slept.

The clock woke him late one wintry afternoon. Sitting up slowly, Bear rubbed his eyes. Then he remembered it was Christmas Eve! His nose was cold and he smelled the fresh snow.

Putting on his scarf and mittens, he went out into the woods, where he found a nice little pine tree. Back home in the candlelight, he decorated his tree. He got an old stocking from his cupboard, and hung it up by his window. Then humming a little tune, Bear fixed his blanket and sat back with his guitar to enjoy the evening.

"There. Everything looks cosy now,

and festive, I believe. I'm so glad I'm wide awake tonight, on Christmas Eve."

He had not been sitting long when he heard a tapping sound at his door. Just a branch in the winter wind, he thought. But then he heard it again. It was a knock. Before Bear could move, the door opened.

"Hello, Bear. I saw your light. I'll warm myself, if that's all right?"

Delighted by this unexpected visitor, Bear got up and invited him in.

"Well, hello stranger, come on in. Don't stand out there and freeze. It's warm inside and you can rest – here, take my blanket, please. I'm only playing my guitar and looking at my tree. But if you've nowhere else to go, do spend some time with me."

So they sat, Bear and his visitor, talking about the snow and the wind, singing a few tunes, and enjoying Christmas Eve. Finally, the little fellow, who was now quite warm, stood and said he really must be going.

"I thank you, Bear, for all you've done. This really has been lots of fun."

Bear stood in the doorway and watched him go off through the forest, thinking what a nice time it had been. All of a sudden his friend shouted back at him.

"Come for a ride, Bear, come with me. I'd really like your company."

A ride! On Christmas Eve! Bear grabbed his scarf and mittens and ran through the deep snow to where a big sleigh sat waiting. The little driver turned as Bear reached the sleigh.

"Just climb up here and hang on tight. You'll be back home before it's light."

Wrapping the big quilt around him, Bear sat down in the seat. Before he could say "LET'S BE OFF", they were off!

Off and up! Up through the air and away into the snowy night . . .

"Oh, what a Christmas!" hollered Bear. "I've never had such fun. I'd like to think that it could be like this for everyone. But most of all, just meeting you has really brought me cheer. Why don't we plan, my little friend, to do this every year?"

So off they flew, far in the night and through the swirling snow, with Bear's companion laughing loud a jolly

HO
HO
HO!

GIFTS

Adèle Geras

It was late on Christmas Eve. Rachel lay in bed, wide awake, wondering why the time went by so slowly when you very much wanted it to go quickly. She had tried all the tricks she could think of for getting to sleep: counting sheep, saying her numbers backwards starting from 100, going through her favourite nursery rhymes, but nothing seemed to work. The landing light made a golden triangle on Rachel's carpet and the ornaments on her chest-of-drawers all had black shadows stretching out behind them.

"I wish," Rachel said aloud, "that there was someone to talk to."

"There is," said a voice. "You can talk to us."

"Who's that?" Rachel sat up in her bed and looked all round the room.

"It's me," said a small wooden camel. "Your camel, up on the chest-of-drawers."

12

"I didn't know you could speak," Rachel said. "Are you quite sure I'm not dreaming?"

"All animals, even ones made of wood and clay and metal, can speak on Christmas Eve," said the camel. "It's the magic in the air. And, of course, the lion lies down with the lamb, and the wolf with the young kid. There are no hunters and hunted on Christmas Eve. All the animals are friends, just for this one night."

"Even cats and mice?"

"Even them."

"And foxes and chickens?" Rachel asked.

"Even them," the camel said.

"How wonderful," said Rachel. "What shall we talk about?"

"I was going to tell all my friends about my great adventure," said the camel.

"Yes, please do," said a tiny copper elephant. "We've all been wondering where you disappeared to. You were gone for a whole week."

"Yes," said a rooster painted all over with red flowers, "one day you were up here with all of us, and the next, you were nowhere to be seen."

"Rachel picked you up," said a porcelain frog, "and ran out of the room. We've been longing to ask you all about it."

"I know where he went," said Rachel. "I'll tell you . . ."

"Ssh!" said a mouse made from a cluster of seashells. "Let Camel tell us himself."

"I went to Rachel's school," said Camel. "All the children in her class were making a Nativity scene to decorate the classroom. Everyone had brought something. One boy brought cotton wool to make clouds out of."

"That was Vivek," said Rachel. "His dad has a chemist's shop."

"Another little girl had pretty material to make clothes out of . . ."

"That was Sharon. Her mother does a lot of sewing," Rachel told the listening animals. "And Patsy brought straw, because she's got a rabbit."

"Marion and Jack brought a lot of plastic farm

14

animals," said Camel. "And Rachel brought me. At first, some of the children thought I shouldn't be in the Nativity scene."

"But then," Rachel interrupted him, "Mrs Ellison explained to the class that there were lots of camels in Bethlehem where Jesus was born, and I told everyone that you'd been sent to me by my grandmother who lives in Jerusalem, as a gift. Jerusalem is very near Bethlehem, so you became very important."

Camel coughed modestly. "I had a little notice pinned to the table beside my feet. It said: 'This camel comes from the Holy Land. It is carved from the wood of the olive tree. Jesus would have seen many olive trees and many camels during His lifetime.' It was a beautiful Nativity scene. Everybody said so."

"Yes, they did," Rachel agreed. "And at the end of term, some of the things we used in the scene were given out as presents. I got one extra sheep, made out of a cotton reel with cotton wool stuck over it. Rukshana gave me the star, which was pinned to the roof of the stable. Look!"

Rachel took the star, which was really a brooch belonging to Rukshana's mother, from its place of honour on her bedside table and held it up for all the animals to see. It glittered in the light and threw small rainbows into the corner of the room.

"How kind of Rukshana!" said the copper elephant. "What a lovely gift! What are you going to give her?"

Rachel hung her head. "I don't know what to give her. I don't even know if her family has gifts at Christmas, and anyway, all the shops are closed now."

"Gifts given at Christmas time are lovely," said the flowered rooster. "It doesn't matter at all whether you always have presents at Christmas or not. I was a Christmas gift myself."

"So was I," said the copper elephant. "I'd only been one of a herd of elephants on the shelf in the Oxfam shop until your father chose me for you. Oh, I was excited! How wonderful to be wrapped in paper with pictures on it, and unwrapped by a real child! Heavenly!"

"But I can't give one of you to Rukshana as a present. I'd miss you," Rachel said.

"What about the toy snowstorm?" asked the porcelain frog. "It's a very pretty ornament. I'm sure anyone would want to have it. You think it's beautiful, don't you?"

Rachel loved the snowstorm. It stood right at the back of the chest-of-drawers, up near the wall and half-hidden by a china pig. Rukshana, whenever she came to play, used to look and look at the way the snowflakes whirled around the little castle, and drifted over the tiny princess who stood in front of it in a long blue and silver dress. Rachel knew she would miss it, but she thought of how happy Rukshana would be when she saw it, and that made her feel better.

"You're brilliant, Frog!" she cried. "I'll wrap it up tomorrow and take it to Rukshana's house. I'll just lie down for a moment, now . . ."

Rachel closed her eyes, and heard, before she fell into a deep sleep, the small voices of her ornaments rising and falling and fading away.

The next afternoon, Rachel took the snowstorm to Rukshana's house. It was wrapped in shiny red paper.

"I've brought you a Christmas present," she said to Rukshana.

"Thank you," said Rukshana, "but I don't really have Christmas presents. We don't really have a proper Christmas."

"But you gave me your mother's brooch. That was a Christmas gift, wasn't it?"

"No," said Rukshana. "That was just a gift given at Christmas time."

"So is this," said Rachel. "I want you to have it."

"Thank you, then," said Rukshana. "What is it?"

"Open it and see."

Rukshana opened the parcel and shook the snowstorm until the flakes filled the air around the castle, and the little princess had almost vanished.

"It's your beautiful ornament!" said Rukshana. "You know I love it. Thank you so much. And look," she pointed over Rachel's head at the iron grey sky. "It's just beginning to snow here. Isn't that lovely? Maybe it's a magic gift. If we stay on the doorstep, we'll look just like the princess."

"But we'll get cold," said Rachel. "I'd rather be a princess indoors."

"Come and play inside, then," said Rukshana.

All afternoon, as the snowflakes fell and floated outside, the two girls pretended that they were wearing blue and silver dresses and living in the little castle in Rukshana's toy snowstorm.

The Story of the Christmas Rose

Scandinavian legend
retold by Norah Montgomerie

Long, long ago there was a Robber family who lived in the Great Forest. Robber Father had stolen sheep and the Bishop had made him an outlaw. So the Robber family went into the forest and there they lived in the shelter of a deep cave, for they had nowhere else to go. Robber Father hunted for food, while Robber Mother and their five children gathered berries to eat, ferns for their beds and wood for the fire.

Sometimes Robber Mother took the children into the village to beg, but they looked so rough and wild with their unkempt hair and their ragged clothes, people were afraid of them and locked their doors when they saw them coming. Sometimes the people left a bundle of old clothes or a parcel of food outside the door for Robber Mother to collect. But not once did they ask her

in or even say a word of greeting, as they did to any stranger. This made Robber Mother furious. She scowled and muttered to herself, even when her sack was full, and looked more fierce than ever.

One warm summer day, as she trudged home, her sack slung over her shoulder, Robber Mother saw that a little door in the monastery wall had

been left open. She stopped and peeped in. There she saw a beautiful garden filled with bright flowers. Honeysuckle, red roses and white jasmine covered the grey stone walls, and she had never seen so many butterflies. She put down her sack and walked into the garden. She bent down to smell the pink roses and smiled.

You can imagine how surprised the monastery gardener was when he saw the rough Robber Mother in his beautiful garden.

"Hi there!" he shouted. "You can't come in here, this is the Abbot's private garden. No women are allowed in here. Be off with you!"

Robber Mother looked up and scowled fiercely.

"I'm doing no harm she snapped, "and I'll go when I've found what I'm looking for."

"You'll go right now, my good woman," shouted the gardener, "or I'll throw you out!"

"Just you try!" laughed Robber Mother, who was much bigger than the gardener and probably stronger too.

This made the gardener very angry. He went off and fetched two fat monks who tried to put her out. But she bit and kicked and screamed, and made such a noise that the old Abbot came hurrying out to see what all the fuss was about.

"This woman won't leave your garden, Lord Abbot," said one of the monks.

"Leave her to me, brothers, I will deal with her," said the Abbot and turning to Robber Mother, he said, "I expect you have never seen such a fine garden, my good woman. Do you want to pick some of the flowers?"

"I do not," said Robber Mother. "This is a fine garden, but it cannot compare with the one we have in the Great Forest every Christmas."

"Is that so?" laughed the Abbot. His garden was his pride and joy and was said to be the finest in the land. But Robber Mother said angrily:

"I'm not joking, Lord Abbot, I know what I'm saying. Every Christmas Eve, part of the Great Forest near our cave is transformed into a wonderful garden to celebrate the birth of the Christ Child. We who live in the forest see it every year. In that garden flowers of all the seasons grow together at the same time, and there are flowers there I would not dare to touch, they are so beautiful. They have frail silver petals and pale gold stamens. We call them Christmas roses. I do not see them in your garden."

The old Abbot listened to Robber Mother. He remembered hearing, as a child, how part of the Great Forest was transformed into a beautiful garden on Christmas Eve. He had longed to see it and then he had forgotten all about it. So he smiled kindly at Robber Mother.

"I have heard of your garden," he said, "and I would like to see it. Would you send one of your children to guide me to the spot next Christmas Eve?"

"How can we be sure you will not drive us away from our cave if we show your where it is?" said Robber Mother.

"I would not do that," said the Abbot. "I would rather ask my Lord Bishop to grant your husband a free pardon in return for your kindness."

"You would do that?" asked Robber Mother eagerly.

"Yes, I shall ask," said the old Abbot, "but whether my Lord Bishop will grant my request I do not know."

"I trust you," said Robber Mother, "and my eldest boy will wait for you next Christmas Eve and guide you through the Great Forest to our cave. He will wait for you by the old oak. But you must promise you will bring only one companion with you – this gardener here."

"I promise," said the Abbot, and after he had blessed the Robber Mother, she left the garden quietly and returned home.

The Abbot went to the Bishop and told him all that had happened, and the story of the Christmas garden. "If God allows the Robber family to see this miracle there must be some good in them. Will you not give the Robber Father a free pardon and a chance to live and work like our people? As it is, their children are growing up rough and wild. If we are not careful we shall have a young Robber gang up there in the Great Forest, and then there will be trouble."

"There is some truth in what you say, good father Abbot," said the Bishop. "Not that I believe this story of the Christmas garden. However, you can go and look for it if you wish, and if you bring me back one of those silver and gold flowers, I'll grant the Robber a free pardon with pleasure."

Well, Christmas Eve came at last. The good old Abbot asked his gardener to go with him into the Great Forest, and there, under the old oak, waited the eldest Robber Son. The gardener muttered angrily under his breath as they followed the boy through the dark forest. He had not wanted to

leave his warm home on Christmas Eve. He thought of his cosy chair beside the fire, and he wished he was sitting in it, watching his wife pluck the turkey and his children decorate the Christmas tree. He did not believe in the Christmas garden and thought the whole expedition was stupid. However, he dared not disobey his old master and he was too fond of him to do so.

On and on they tramped through the snow till they came to a cave. They followed the boy through an opening into a cavern where the Robber Mother was sitting beside a log fire. The Robber children sprawled about the floor playing with small stones, while Robber Father lay stretched out on a pile of dried bracken.

"Sit down by the fire and warm yourself, Lord Abbot," said Robber Mother. "You can sleep if you're tired. I'll keep watch and I'll wake you when it is time to see what you have come to see."

"I'll keep watch too," said the gardener, who still did not trust the Robber family.

The old Abbot thanked the woman and stretched himself on the ground beside the fire and fell asleep. He was so tired.

He had not slept long when he woke to hear the chimes of the Christmas bells. The gardener helped him to his feet and they followed the Robber family to the entrance of the cave.

"It is extraordinary to be able to hear the Christmas bells here in the forest. I wouldn't have thought it possible," said the Abbot.

"Ah well, everything looks the same as ever out here," grumbled the gardener, who was still in a bad temper.

It was true, the forest was as dark and gloomy as before, but instead of an icy wind, they felt a warm gentle breeze and a strange stirring all about them. Suddenly the bells stopped ringing. And then it happened.

The darkness turned into a pink dawn. The snow melted from the ground, leaving emerald shoots that grew before their eyes. Ferns sent up their fronds, curled like a bishop's staff, and spring flowers carpeted the earth. Trees burst into leaf and then into blossom. Butterflies and birds darted from tree to tree, and there was a soft hum of insects.

The Robber children laughed and rolled in the grass while Robber Mother and Robber Father stared wide-eyed and smiling. They too seemed transformed. And there, at his feet, the Abbot saw the silver and gold flower of the Christmas rose. He was filled with happiness and he knelt down and thanked God for allowing him to see such a miracle.

This seemed to make the gardener more angry than ever.

"This is no miracle," he said in a loud voice, "this is witchcraft and the work of the devil!"

As he said this darkness fell and an icy wind blew snow through the forest. The Robber family ran shivering into the cave, but the old Abbot stumbled forward on his face, clutching at the earth as he fell. The garden vanished, leaving the forest as dark and gloomy as ever.

The gardener hoisted the Abbot on to his back and carried him back to the monastery. There he was laid on his bed. The monks all marvelled at the radiant smile on his still face. At least he had died with a happy heart, they told each other.

Now, the old Abbot was found to have the root of a plant clutched in one hand. It was given to the gardener who planted it carefully in the Abbot's garden. Every day he went to see if it was growing, but although there were green leaves there were no signs of a flower in the spring, nor in the summer, and autumn passed and there was not even a bud to be seen. The gardener wondered if it would ever flower.

Then on Christmas morning, when the ground was sprinkled with snow, the gardener saw a beautiful cluster of silvery white flowers growing from the plant, their frail petals surrounding the pale golden stamens. He had seen the flower only once before, in that Christmas garden of the Great Forest. It must be the Christmas rose, and the good Abbot had managed to pluck one after all.

At once the gardener knew what he must do. He picked three of the white flowers and took them to the Bishop.

"My Lord Bishop," said the gardener, "our father Abbot sends you these flowers as he promised." Then he told the Bishop about the wonderful Christmas garden and all that had happened in the Great Forest that Christmas Eve.

"The good Abbot kept his promise and I shall keep mine," said the Bishop, and he wrote a free pardon for the Robber Father there and then.

The gardener took the pardon to the Robber Father but when he reached the cave he found the entrance barred against him.

"Go away!" roared Robber Father. "Thanks to you there was no wonderful garden here this Christmas Eve. Go away, unless you want a fight!"

"You're right, it was my fault; I had no faith. I was wrong but you must allow me to deliver your free pardon from the Bishop. You are free, and from now on you may return to the village and live and work among the people."

And so it was that the Robber family left the Great Forest and were able to enjoy Christmas in their own home, with all their friends around them.

A PRESENT FOR SANTA CLAUS

Carolyn Haywood

There were many signs that Christmas would soon be here. At night the main street looked like fairyland. Tiny electric lights were strung all over the branches of the bare trees. The children talked of Santa Claus and when they would go to see him.

One Saturday morning when Star came into the kitchen for her breakfast, she said to her mother, "Today's the day, isn't it? I'm going to see Santa Claus!"

"That's right," her mother replied.

"When will we go?" Star asked as she sat down to eat her bowl of oatmeal.

"We'll go as soon as I finish clearing up the kitchen," her mother replied.

As soon as Star finished her breakfast, she said, "I'll put my things on and feed the turtles." Star had two turtles that she had named Mabel and Marble.

Star went into her room. She kept her turtles in a glass tank. She picked up a box of turtle food and sprinkled it around the turtles. Then she scratched their backs and said, "Now eat your breakfast. I'm going to see Santa Claus."

When Star and her mother were ready to leave, Star was wearing her blue snow pants and her warm red jacket and cap. Just as her mother opened the door Star cried out, "Oh Mummy! I haven't any present for Santa Claus."

"You don't take a present to Santa Claus, Star," her mother said. "Santa Claus brings presents to you."

"Oh, but I want a present for him," said Star.

"Now, Star!" said her mother. "Nobody takes presents to Santa Claus."

"But it's Christmas," said Star. "Everybody takes everybody a present."

"Everybody does not take everybody a present," said her mother. "Now come along."

Star shook her head. "Everybody should take Santa Claus a present, because he gives presents to everybody's children. I have to take him a present. Maybe he's like me. Maybe it's his birthday."

Star's mother sat down on the chair beside the door. She held her head and said, "Darling! It is *not* Santa Claus's birthday. You don't have a present for him, you don't need a present for him, and he doesn't want a present."

"Everybody wants presents, Mummy," said Star, almost in tears. "I'll go and find something." She darted up the stairs.

She wasn't gone long. When she came down she had a satisfied look on her face. "I'm going to give Mabel to Santa Claus," she said.

"Mabel!" her mother exclaimed. "What will Santa Claus do with Mabel?"

"He'll love Mabel," Star replied.

Star's mother shook her head. "Come along," she said, opening the door. She took Star's hand and hurried her to the bus stop.

When they were seated in the bus, her mother said, "Where is Mabel?"

"In my pocket," Star replied. "In the pocket of my snow pants."

"I hope Mabel's happy in your pocket," her

mother said. "It doesn't seem to be the best place for a little turtle."

"She's all right," said Star. "I put my hand in and tickle her every once in a while. Mabel likes being tickled."

"You're sure you want to give her away?" her mother asked. "You've been very fond of your turtles."

"Well, I didn't have time to find anything else for a present for Santa Claus," said Star, "so I went over to Mabel and I said, 'Mabel, you're going to be a present for Santa Claus.' Then I said, 'I guess you don't know about Santa Claus, but he's not a turtle.' "

Star looked up at her mother. "I wanted Mabel to know that he isn't a turtle, so she won't be surprised when she sees him. I told her he's a sort of magic person. And you know something, Mummy?"

"What?" her mother asked.

"Well, once in a fairy story a frog got turned into a handsome prince, so maybe Santa Claus can turn Mabel into a beautiful princess." Star turned and gazed out the window. "She'd be Princess Mabel!" she said with a sigh.

Star's mother sighed, too. Then she said, "I don't believe turning turtles into princesses is exactly Santa Claus's line. He's very busy in the toy business."

Star poked her finger into her pocket and tickled Mabel. "Well, I think I'll call her Princess Mabel anyway."

When Star and her mother reached the store, they went directly to the toy department, where they found Santa Claus. Star stood holding her mother's hand and stared at Santa Claus. There he sat in a big chair on a platform. He looked magnificent in his bright red suit trimmed with white fur and his shiny black boots. He held a little boy on his knee. Star saw the boy whisper into Santa Claus's ear, and she saw Santa Claus's white teeth when he laughed and put the little boy down.

There were several children standing in a line waiting to speak to Santa Claus. Star's mother took her to the end of the line and said, "You wait here

until it's your turn to speak to Santa Claus."

"You'll wait with me, won't you, Mummy?" Star asked.

"I'll stand nearby," her mother replied.

"Where shall I put my present for Santa Claus?" Star asked. "He doesn't have any Christmas tree."

"Well, you certainly couldn't hang Mabel on a Christmas tree, even if he had one," said her mother. "You see, Star, none of these children have presents for Santa Claus."

"That's because they forgot," said Star as she moved forward in the line.

Star watched as the children ahead of her reached Santa Claus. Some he took on his lap and

some stood by his knee. When the little boy ahead of her began to talk to Santa Claus, Star put her hand into her pocket. She was surprised, for she couldn't find Mabel. She thought perhaps she had forgotten which pocket she had put her in, so she dug into her other one. Mabel was not there.

Now the little boy had gone, and Santa Claus was beckoning to Star. She was still poking around in her pocket when she reached his knee.

"Hello!" said Santa Claus in his big, cheery voice. "What's your name?"

"I'm Star," she replied, just as her finger went through a hole in her pocket.

Santa Claus leaned over and said, "What seems to be the matter?"

"I brought you a present," Star replied, "but I can't find it." Star dug down and made the hole in her pocket bigger.

"What is it you're trying to find?" Santa Claus asked.

"Mabel!" Star replied.

"Oh!" said Santa Claus.

"I guess she fell through the hole in my pocket," said Star, leaning over like a jackknife. Then she unzipped the bottom of the leg of her snow pants. She straightened up and said, "I'll shake my leg, and maybe she'll fall out."

"That's the thing!" said Santa Claus. "Shake a leg!"

Star shook and then she jumped while everyone

38

stood around and watched her. Mabel did not appear. "I'll find her," said Star. "She's hiding!"

Star sat down on the floor beside Santa Claus's big black boots. She felt inside the leg of her pants and suddenly her face broke into a wide smile. "I found her!" she said, looking up at Santa Claus.

"Good!" said Santa Claus. "I can't wait to see Mabel."

Star leaned against Santa Claus's knee. "Hold out your hand," she said. Santa Claus held out his big hand, and Star placed the tiny turtle on her back in his palm. "I hope she's all right," said Star. "If she kicks her legs, she's alive."

Santa Claus's great big head in his red cap bent over his hand as Star leaned against him. Their heads were together as they watched to see if Mabel would kick her legs. Suddenly Star cried out, "She's alive! Mabel's alive!"

"Sure enough!" said Santa Claus. "She's alive and kicking!"

Star looked up into Santa Claus's face. "I'm sorry I couldn't wrap up your present, " she said. "You don't mind if Mabel isn't wrapped up, do you?"

Santa Claus drew Star to him and gave her a great big hug. "I never had a nicer present than Mabel," he said. "Thank you, and a merry Christmas to you."

As she walked away Star turned and looked back at Santa Claus. He waved his hand. Star waved too

and called back, "Mabel likes hamburger! Just a teenie-weenie bit, of course."

"I'll remember," Santa Claus promised. "Hamburger for her Christmas dinner!"

On Christmas morning, when Star went to the fireplace in the living room, standing on the hearth was a beautiful doll dressed like a princess with a crown on her head. A card stood beside her. It said:

This is Princess Mabel, from Santa Claus.

THE MICE AND THE CHRISTMAS TREE

Alf Prøysen

Now you shall hear the story about a family of mice who lived behind the larder wall.

Every Christmas Eve, Mother Mouse and the children swept and dusted their whole house with their tails, and for a Christmas tree Father Mouse decorated an old boot with spider's web instead of tinsel. For Christmas presents, the children were each given a little nut, and Mother Mouse held up a piece of bacon fat for them all to sniff.

After that, they danced round and round the boot, and sang and played games till they were tired out. Then Father Mouse would say, "That's all for tonight! Time to go to bed!"

That is how it had been every Christmas and that is how it was to be this year. The little mice held each other by the tail and danced round the boot, while Granny Mouse enjoyed the fun from her rocking-chair, which wasn't a rocking-chair at all, but a small turnip.

But when Father Mouse said, "That's all for tonight! Time to go to bed!" all the children dropped each other's tails and shouted: "No! No!"

"What's that?" said Father Mouse. "When I say it's time for bed, it's time for bed!"

"We don't want to!" cried the children, and hid behind Granny's turnip rocking-chair.

"What's all this nonsense?" said Mother Mouse. "Christmas is over now, so off you go, the lot of you!"

"No, no!" wailed the children, and climbed on to Granny's knee. She hugged them all lovingly.

"Why don't you want to go to bed, my little sugar lumps?"

"Because we want to go upstairs to the big drawing-room and dance round a proper Christmas tree," said the eldest Mouse child. "You see, I've been peeping through a crack in the wall and I saw a huge Christmas tree with lots and lots of lights on it."

"We want to see the Christmas tree and all the lights too!" shouted the other children.

"Oh, but the drawing-room can be a very dangerous place for mice," said Granny.

"Not when all the people have gone to bed," objected the eldest Mouse child.

"Oh, do let's go!" they all pleaded.

Mother and Father Mouse didn't know what to say, but they couldn't very well disappoint the children on Christmas Eve.

"Perhaps we could take them up there just for a minute or two," suggested Mother Mouse.

"Very well," said Father, "but follow me closely."

So they set off. They tiptoed past three tins of herring, two large jars of honey, and a cider barrel.

"We have to go very carefully here," whispered Father Mouse, "not to knock over any bottles. Are you all right, Granny?"

"Of course I'm all right," said Granny. "You just carry on. I haven't been up in the drawing-room since I was a little Mouse girl; it'll be fun to see it all again."

"Mind the trap!" said the eldest Mouse child. "It's behind that sack of potatoes."

"I know that," said Granny. "It's been there since I was a child. I'm not afraid of that!" And she took a flying leap right over the trap and scuttled after the others up the wall.

"What a lovely tree!" cried all the children when they peeped out of the hole by the drawing-room fireplace. "But where are the lights? You said there'd be lots and lots of lights, didn't you? Didn't you?" the children shouted, crowding round the eldest one, who was quite sure there had been lights the day before.

They stood looking for a little while. Then

suddenly a whole lot of coloured lights lit up the tree! Do you know what had happened? By accident, Granny had touched the electric switch by the fireplace.

"Oh, how lovely!" they all exclaimed, and Father and Mother and Granny thought it was very nice too. They walked right round the tree, looking at the decorations, the little paper baskets, the glass balls, and the glittering tinsel garlands. But the children found something even more exciting: a mechanical lorry!

Of course, they couldn't wind it up themselves, but its young master had wound it up before he went to bed, to be ready for him to play with in the morning. So when the Mouse children clambered into it, it started off right away.

"Children, children! You mustn't make such a noise!" warned Mother Mouse.

But the children didn't listen; they were having a wonderful time going round and round and round in the lorry.

"As long as the cat doesn't come!" said Father Mouse anxiously.

He had hardly spoken before the cat walked silently through the open door.

Father, Mother and Granny Mouse all made a dash for the hole in the skirting but the children were trapped in the lorry, which just went on going round and round and round. They had never been so scared in all their Mouse lives.

The cat crouched under the tree, and every time the lorry passed she tried to tap it with her front paw. But it was going too fast and she missed.

Then the lorry started slowing down. "I think we'd better make a jump for it and try to get up the tree," said the eldest Mouse. So when the lorry stopped they all gave a big jump and landed on the branches of the tree.

One hid in a paper basket, another behind a bulb (which nearly burned him), a third swung on a glass ball, and the fourth rolled himself up in some cotton wool. But where was the eldest Mouse? Oh yes, he had climbed right to the top and was balancing next to the star and shouting at the cat:

Silly, silly cat
You can't catch us!
You're much too fat,
Silly, silly cat!

But the cat pretended not to hear or see the little mice. She sharpened her claws on the lorry.

"I'm not interested in catching mice tonight," she said as if to herself. "I've been waiting for a chance to play with this lorry all day."

"Pooh! That's just a story!" said the eldest who was also the bravest. "You'd catch us quick enough if we came down."

"No, I wouldn't. Not on Christmas Eve!" said the cat. And she kept to her word. When they did all come timidly down, she never moved, but just said: "Hurry back to your hole, children. Christmas Eve is the one night when I'm kind to little mice. But woe betide you if I catch you tomorrow morning!"

The little mice pelted through that hole and never stopped running till they got to their home behind the larder wall. There were Father and

Mother and Granny Mouse waiting in fear and trembling to know what had happened to them.

When Mother Mouse had heard their story she said, "You must promise me, children, never to go up to the drawing-room again."

"We promise! We promise!" they all shouted together. Then she made them say after her The Mouse Law, which they'd all been taught when they were tiny:

We promise always to obey
Our parents dear in every way,
To wipe our feet upon the mat
And, never, never cheek the cat.

Remember too the awful danger
Of taking money from a stranger;
We will not go off on our own
Or give our mother cause to moan.

Odd bits of cheese and bacon-scraps
Are almost certain to be traps,
So we must look for bigger things
Like loaves and cakes and doughnut-rings;

And if these rules we still obey
We'll live to run another day.

RAMONA AND THE THREE WISE PERSONS

Beverly Cleary

Suddenly, a few days before Christmas when the Quimby family least expected it, the telephone rang for Ramona's father. He had a job! The morning after New Year's Day he was to report for training as a checker in a chain of supermarkets. The pay was good, he would have to work some evenings, and maybe someday he would get to manage a market!

After that telephone call Mr Quimby stopped reaching for cigarettes that were not there and began to whistle as he ran the vacuum cleaner and folded the clothes from the dryer. The worried frown disappeared from Mrs Quimby's forehead.

Beezus looked even more calm and serene. Ramona, however, made a mistake. She told her mother about her tight shoes. Mrs Quimby then wasted a Saturday afternoon shopping for shoes when she could have been sewing on Ramona's costume for the Christmas pageant. As a result, when they drove to church the night of the Christmas programme, Ramona was the only unhappy member of the family.

Mrs Quimby leaned back, tired but relaxed. Beezus smiled her gentle Virgin Mary

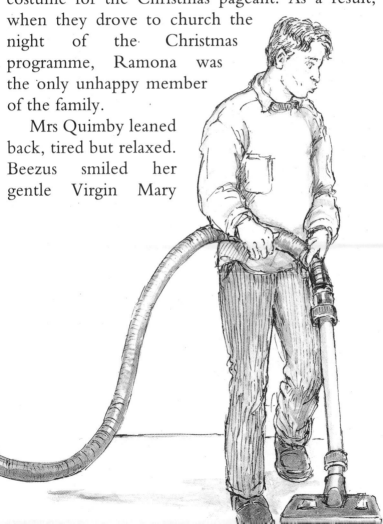

pageant smile that Ramona had found so annoying for the past three weeks.

Ramona sulked.

Mr Quimby sang, "Oh, I feel like shouting in my heart . . ."

Ramona interrupted her father's song. "I don't care what anybody says," she burst out. "If I can't be a good sheep, I am not going to be a sheep at all." She yanked off the white terry-cloth headdress with pink-lined ears that she was wearing and stuffed it into the pocket of her car coat. She

started to pull her father's rolled-down socks from her hands because they didn't really look like hooves, but then she decided they kept her hands warm. She squirmed on the lumpy terry-cloth tail sewn to the seat of her pyjamas. Ramona could not pretend that faded pyjamas printed with an army of pink rabbits, half of them upside down, made her look like a sheep, and Ramona was usually good at pretending.

Mrs Quimby's voice was tired. "Ramona, your tail and headdress were all I could manage, and I had to stay up late last night to finish those. I simply don't have time for complicated sewing."

Ramona knew that. Her family had been telling her so for the past three weeks.

"A sheep should be woolly," said Ramona. "A sheep should not be printed with pink bunnies."

"You can be a sheep that has been shorn," said Mr Quimby, who was full of jokes now that he was going to work again. "Or how about a wolf in sheep's clothing?"

"You just want me to be miserable," said Ramona, not appreciating her father's humour and feeling that everyone in her family should be miserable because she was.

"She's worn out," said Mrs Quimby, as if Ramona could not hear. "It's so hard to wait for Christmas at her age."

Ramona raised her voice. "I am *not* worn out! You know sheep don't wear pyjamas."

"That's showbiz," said Mr Quimby.

"Daddy!" Beezus-Mary was shocked. "It's church!"

The sight of light shining through the stained-glass window of the big stone church diverted Ramona for a moment. The window looked beautiful, as if it were made of jewels.

Mr Quimby backed the car into a parking space. "Ho-ho-ho!" he said as he turned off the ignition. "'Tis the season to be jolly."

Jolly was the last thing Ramona was going to be.

Leaving the car, she stooped down inside her car coat to hide as many rabbits as possible. Black branches clawed at the rain-filled sky, and the wind was raw.

"Stand up straight," said Ramona's heartless father.

"I'll get wet," said Ramona. "I might catch cold, and then you'd be sorry."

"Run between the drops," said Mr Quimby.

"They're too close together," answered Ramona.

"Oh, you two," said Mrs Quimby with a tired little laugh as she backed out of the car and tried to open her umbrella at the same time.

"I will not be in it," Ramona defied her family once and for all. "They can give the programme without me."

Her father's answer was a surprise. "Suit yourself," he said. "You're not going to spoil our evening."

Mrs Quimby gave the seat of Ramona's pyjamas an affectionate pat. "Run along, little lamb, wagging your tail behind you."

Ramona walked stiff-legged so that her tail would not wag.

At the church door the family parted, the girls going downstairs to the Sunday-school room, which was a confusion of chattering children piling coats and raincoats on chairs. Ramona found a corner behind the Christmas tree, where Santa would pass out candy canes after the programme. She sat down on the floor with her car coat pulled over her bent knees.

Nobody noticed Ramona. Everyone was having too much fun. Shepherds found their cloaks, which were made from old cotton bedspreads. Beezus's friend, Henry Huggins, arrived and put on the dark robe he was to wear in the part of Joseph.

The other two sheep appeared. Howie's acrylic sheep suit, with the zipper on the front, was as thick and as fluffy as Ramona knew it would be. Ramona longed to pet Howie; he looked so soft. Davy's flannel suit was fastened with safety pins, and

there was something wrong about the ears. If his tail had been longer, he could have passed for a kitten, but he did not seem to mind. Both boys wore brown mittens. Davy, who was a thin little sheep, jumped up and down to make his tail wag, which surprised Ramona. At school he was always so shy. Maybe he felt brave inside his sheep suit. Howie, a chunky sheep, made his tail wag, too. My ears are as good as theirs, Ramona told herself. The floor felt cold through the seat of her thin pyjamas.

"Look at the little lambs!" cried an angel. "Aren't they darling?"

"Ba-a, ba-a!" bleated Davy and Howie.

Ramona longed to be there with them, jumping and ba-a-ing and wagging her tail, too. Maybe the faded rabbits didn't show as much as she had thought. She sat hunched and miserable. She had told her father she would *not* be a sheep, and she couldn't back down now. She hoped God was too busy to notice her, and then she changed her mind. Please, God, prayed Ramona, in case He wasn't too busy to listen to a miserable little sheep, I don't really mean to be horrid. It just works out that way. She was

frightened, she discovered, for when the programme began, she would be left alone in the church basement. The lights might even be turned out, a scary thought, for the big stone church filled Ramona with awe, and she did not want to be left alone in the dark with her awe. Please, God, prayed Ramona, get me out of this mess.

Beezus, in a long blue robe with a white scarf over her head and carrying a baby's blanket and a big flashlight, found her little sister. "Come out, Ramona," she coaxed. "Nobody will notice your costume. You know Mother would have made you a whole sheep suit if she had time. Be a good sport. Please."

Ramona shook her head and blinked to keep tears from falling. "I told Daddy I wouldn't be in the programme, and I won't."

"Well, okay, if that's the way you feel," said Beezus, forgetting to act like Mary. She left her little sister to her misery.

Ramona sniffed and wiped her eyes on her hoof. Why didn't some grown-up come along and *make* her join the other sheep? No grown-up came. No one seemed to remember there were supposed to be three sheep, not even Howie, who played with her almost every day.

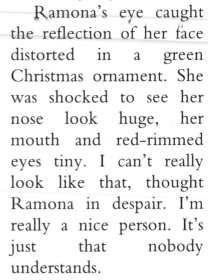

Ramona's eye caught the reflection of her face distorted in a green Christmas ornament. She was shocked to see her nose look huge, her mouth and red-rimmed eyes tiny. I can't really look like that, thought Ramona in despair. I'm really a nice person. It's just that nobody understands.

Ramona mopped her eyes on her hoof again, and as she did she noticed three big girls, so tall they were probably in the eighth grade, putting on robes made from better bedspreads than the shepherd's

robes. That's funny, she thought. Nothing she had
learned in Sunday school told her anything about
girls in long robes in the Nativity scene. Could they
be Jesus's aunts?

One of the girls began to dab tan cream from a
little jar on her face and to smear it around while
another girl held up a pocket mirror. The third girl,
holding her own mirror, used an eyebrow pencil to
give herself heavy brows.

Makeup, thought Ramona with interest,

wishing she could wear it. The girls took turns darkening their faces and brows. They looked like different people.

One of the girls noticed her. "Hi, there," she said. "Why are you hiding back there?"

"Because," was Ramona's all-purpose answer. "Are you Jesus's aunts?" she asked.

The girls found the question funny. "No," answered one. "We're the Three Wise Persons."

Ramona was puzzled. "I thought they were supposed to be wise *men*," she said.

"The boys backed out at the last minute," explained the girl with the blackest eyebrows. "Mrs Russo said women can be wise, too, so tonight we are the Three Wise Persons."

This idea seemed like a good one to Ramona, who wished she were big enough to be a wise person hiding behind makeup so nobody would know who she was.

"Are you supposed to be in the programme?" asked one of the girls.

"I was supposed to be a sheep, but I changed my mind," said Ramona, changing it back again. She pulled out her sheep headdress and put it on.

"Isn't she adorable?" said one of the wise persons.

Ramona was surprised. She had never been called adorable before. Bright, lively, yes; adorable, no. She smiled and felt more lovable. Maybe pink-lined ears helped.

"Why don't you want to be a sheep?" asked a wise person.

Ramona had an inspiration. "Because I don't have any makeup."

"Makeup on a *sheep*!" exclaimed a wise person, and giggled.

Ramona persisted. "Sheep have black noses," she hinted. "Maybe I could have a black nose."

The girls looked at one another. "Don't tell my mother," said one, "but I have some mascara. We could make her nose black."

"Please!" begged Ramona, getting to her feet and coming out from behind the Christmas tree.

The owner of the mascara fumbled in her shoulder bag, which was hanging on a chair, and brought out a tiny box. "Let's go in the kitchen where there's a sink," she said, and when Ramona followed her, she moistened an elf-sized brush, which she rubbed on the mascara in the box.

Then she began to brush it onto Ramona's nose. It tickled, but Ramona held still. "It feels like brushing my teeth only on my nose," she remarked. The wise person stood back to look at her work and then applied another coat of mascara to Ramona's nose. "There," she said at last. "Now you look like a real sheep."

Ramona felt like a real sheep. "Ba-a-a," she bleated, a sheep's way of saying thank you. Ramona felt so much better, she could almost pretend she was woolly. She peeled off her coat and found that the faded pink rabbits really didn't show much in the dim light. She pranced off among the angels, who had been handed little flashlights, which they were supposed to hold like

candles. Instead they were shining them into their mouths to show one another how weird they looked with light showing through their cheeks. The other two sheep stopped jumping when they saw her.

"You don't look like Ramona," said Howie.

"B-a-a. I'm not Ramona. I'm a sheep." The boys did not say one word about Ramona's pyjamas. They wanted black noses too, and when Ramona told them where she got hers, they ran off to find the wise persons. When they returned, they no longer looked like Howie and Davy in sheep suits. They looked like strangers in sheep suits. So I must really look like somebody else, thought Ramona with increasing happiness. Now she

could be in the programme, and her parents wouldn't know because they wouldn't recognize her.

"B-a-a!" bleated three prancing, black-nosed sheep. "B-a-a, b-a-a."

Mrs Russo clapped her hands. "Quiet, everybody!" she ordered. "All right, Mary and Joseph up by the front stairs. Shepherds and sheep next and then wise persons. Angels line up by the back stairs."

Ramona's heart began to pound as if something exciting were about to happen. Up the stairs she tiptoed and through the arched door. The only light came from candelabra on either side of the chancel and from a streetlight shining through a stained-glass window. Ramona had never seen the church look so beautiful or so mysterious.

Beezus sat down on a low stool in the centre of the chancel and arranged the baby's blanket around the flashlight. Henry stood behind her. The sheep got down on their hands and knees in front of the shepherds, and the Three Wise Persons stood off to one side, holding bath-salts jars that looked as if they really could hold frankincense and myrrh.

A shivery feeling ran down Ramona's backbone, as if magic were taking place. She looked up at Beezus, smiling tenderly down at the flashlight, and it seemed as if Baby Jesus really could be inside the blanket.

Then Ramona found her parents in the second

row. They were smiling gently, proud of Beezus. This gave Ramona an aching feeling inside. They would not know her in her makeup. Maybe they would think she was some other sheep, and she didn't want to be some other sheep. She wanted to be their sheep. She wanted them to be proud of her, too.

Ramona saw her father look away from Beezus and look directly at her. Did he recognize her? Yes, he did. Mr Quimby winked. Ramona was shocked.

Winking in church! How could her father do such a thing? He winked again and this time held up his thumb and forefinger in a circle. Ramona understood. Her father was telling her he was proud of her, too.

Ramona was filled with joy. Christmas was the most beautiful, magic time of the whole year. Her parents loved her, and she loved them, and Beezus, too. At home there was a Christmas tree and under it, presents, fewer than at past Christmases, but presents all the same. Ramona could not contain her feelings. "B-a-a," she bleated joyfully.

She felt the nudge of a shepherd's crook on the seat of her pyjamas and heard her shepherd whisper through clenched teeth, "You be quiet!" Ramona did not bleat again. She wiggled her seat to make her tail wag.

CHRISTMAS THROUGH A KNOTHOLE

Katherine Gibson

Old Hans was the best wood-carver in all the land. But just three weeks before Christmas, he was thrown into jail! Again and again he had been told not to hunt in the king's own hunting ground. But Hans's mouth would water for the taste of roast rabbit, and to the king's lands he would go and set his traps. This time, alas, Hans was caught.

The jailer was a kind man. Since Hans was old, he let him have a fire and some wood to carve. But Hans was very unhappy. To be in jail on Christmas, when all the village was making merry!

Hans lived all alone, but he had a good friend named Gretchen. Gretchen was seven years old and had big grey eyes and long, smooth, yellow hair in two pigtails. Gretchen also had a little brother named Max. He was as round and brown as she was pink and white. He was as naughty and full of laughter as she was quiet and thoughtful.

"Oh, Max," Gretchen said to her brother, "what shall we do? Poor Uncle Hans is in jail, just for hunting rabbits. He always has his Christmas dinner with us. Now he won't have any – not a bite."

"And worse than that," said Max, "we won't get any toys!" For every year, of course, Old Hans carved the most wonderful toys for them.

Max looked cross. Gretchen looked sad. They walked past the jail. Like all the other houses in the village, it was made of wood. The walls were very thick, and the only window was far, far above their heads.

Suddenly Max said, "Look, there is a hole."

It was a large knothole in the wood. Max stood on his tiptoes and put his eye to the hole. "I can see him. I can see Old Hans. He is carving, just the way he always does!"

"Oh, Max, let me see!" cried Gretchen. She bent down, and sure enough she could see Old Hans – or part of him.

Max took out his pocket knife (every boy in the village carried a knife) and scratched at the hole until he made it bigger. Then he put his lips to the hole and called, "Hans, Uncle Hans, come here! Come to the knothole!"

Old Hans was surprised. He got up and followed the sound of the excited small voice.

70

The children told him all the village news. In turn, he told them how long the days were in jail.

"It will be a sad Christmas for you, Uncle Hans," said Gretchen. "We will miss you at home."

"For us it will be even worse." Max was almost crying. "We won't have any toys – not one!"

"You come back here tomorrow," Uncle Hans said.

The children could hardly wait for the next day. In the morning, they hurried back to the knothole. "Here we are, here we are, Uncle Hans," they shouted

The knothole was bigger now. Out of it, Uncle Hans pushed a tiny wooden figure. It was a little boy carrying a flower in his hand.

"Oh," cried Max, "it is just like me!"

"Only you never carry flowers," said Gretchen. "You just carry big sticks."

The next day, a fat duck came through the knothole. Then a market woman. "Why," said Gretchen, "that is old Martha!"

Day after day, the tiny carved figures came through the knothole. At last the children had a whole village. And not one toy was more than three inches high.

"Uncle Hans has done so much for us," said Gretchen. "I wonder, can we make him a knothole Christmas dinner?"

They talked with their mother. And this is what

they did. They wrapped some fine pieces of roast goose into long thin bundles, four of them. They took some long, thin sausages that Hans liked ever so much. Gretchen baked some rolls. They were a very funny shape, not very different from the sausages, long and thin. Even the Christmas cakes were rolled up tight, with sugar and nuts inside.

"And a tall, thin candle – a Christmas candle. I will make it myself," said Max. And he did.

Christmas Eve came. There was snow on the pointed roofs of the houses, and on the pointed tops of the fir trees. Just as the lights were lit,

Max and Gretchen went to the jail.

They called Old Hans. He came and gave them the prettiest toy of all. It was a funny, fat, little fellow with a star on his head – a Christmas angel. Then Max pushed, and Gretchen pushed, and soon Hans's Christmas dinner was inside the jail. Last of all, Max pushed through the candle.

"Made it myself!" he said proudly, jumping up and down.

The children said they had never had such toys, never. And they loved them because they were so tiny. And Hans said the best dinner he ever had was the Christmas dinner through a knothole.

THE LITTLE
FIR TREE

Hans Christian Andersen
retold by Alison Carter

A nna pulled her boots on hard and stumped
outdoors.

"I don't want to go to school tomorrow!" she
thought crossly. "I want it to be Christmas again.
It's not fair... it went so fast, and now there's
another whole year to wait!" She looked about at
the damp brown garden. All dead. Her mother had
said she might find the first snowdrop coming up if
she looked very hard, and she did want to.

Suddenly something bright and golden caught
her eye. In a corner of the garden stood the
Christmas tree, where someone had thrown it on
twelfth night, with its golden star still on the top.

"Oh good, I can have it for dressing up," she
said, pulling the star off the prickly little tree. And
then she said, "Poor tree, all bare and cold."

"Mmm..." sighed the tree; it was just green

enough to speak still. "I'm a poor bare tree, thrown outside, and now my star's gone too, like everything else."

"Oh, don't be sad," said Anna kindly. "Think how pretty you were at Christmas, all sparkling and green."

"Yes," answered the tree wistfully, "I was very fine, wasn't I, all lit up day and night, with my coloured lights, and tiny toys, and shiny sweets and golden decorations? The children loved me,

76

just like the sparrows said they would."

"Which sparrows?" asked Anna, curious to hear the tree's story.

"The sparrows in the forest when I was one year old. I was green and alive and growing then, and I didn't realize how lucky I was to be at home with my family. The sparrows had been to the

farmhouse nearby at Christmas time, and had peeped in at the windows. 'There's a fir tree in there,' they twittered excitedly, 'but you'd hardly recognize it. It's covered in tinsel, lights and little presents, and on the top there is a golden star. The children think it's the most beautiful tree in the whole world.' From that moment, I only wanted one thing: to be a Christmas tree. I couldn't wait to grow big enough. And I never took any notice of what the sun said to me!" whispered the tree.

"The sun? What did the sun say?" asked Anna.

" 'Gently now, little one,' he warned in his kind smiling voice. 'You're still young; enjoy yourself while you can. Feel my warmth on your branches; feel the soft rain kissing your boughs, stretch and bend in the wind.' But all that just made me cross . . . who'd want to be stuck in a forest when they could be decorated and admired like that other fir tree?"

"I've always wanted to go to a real forest," said Anna. "Didn't you like it there?"

"No, I didn't, because I was the smallest – even when I stretched – and children used to point at me and say what a dear little tree I was, and the hare used to jump right over me, just to make it worse." The little fir tree sounded quite cross still, even though it had all happened so long ago.

"Oh, but aren't you lucky," cried Anna, trying to cheer the tree a little, "I've never seen a real hare."

"I didn't see it like that then," said the tree softly. "I couldn't wait to grow big like the others. Next year the woodman came and chose the tallest trees for ships' masts. How wonderful, I thought, they'll see the world. When shall I grow tall enough to be a mast and see the world?"

"But you never did, did you?" said Anna.

"No," whispered the forlorn tree, its voice dry and cracked, "I just waited impatiently there; waiting, waiting without seeing. The soft cold snow piled up on my branches; then the spring rain splashed down on me, and the sun warmed me. But I was just waiting for that woodman to come and choose me to be a Christmas tree, to be beautiful and admired." The fir tree sighed again, then remembered something else. "And do you know, the thrush chose me to hold her nest for her one spring, brushing through my needles, in and out, in and out, making her nest. And I sheltered her little ones . . ."

"You were very lucky," said Anna.

"Yes I was, but all I could think of was Christmas, Christmas, and the wonderful things the sparrows had told me about when I was little. I couldn't wait for the woodman to come back and choose me."

"And then what happened?" asked Anna, who was pressed right up close to the poor, prickly little brown tree so she could hear.

"And then," the poor tree sighed, "the

80

woodman came at last, swinging his sharp axe. When he saw me, he said, 'There's a good one!' How proud I was, how excited, my dreams were coming true! Then he swung his axe, and felled me.

How sudden it was, what cold cruel metal! I flung out my branches, but it was no use, and I crashed down hurt and dizzy." The tree was silent for a moment, and then went on more cheerfully.

"Next thing I knew I was in a warm room in a tub, and your mother was saying what a lovely tree I was. She hung me with shiny baubles that tickled my branches; and the lights, they were a bit hot, but so pretty. And then you came in with your friends, and you looked so pleased. I really bristled with pride because you all loved me so. And you danced and sang, and opened presents, and pulled the sweets off my branches: how tightly I was holding them!"

Anna put her arms round the little tree, who had once been so proud and green.

"So you did enjoy Christmas after all," she said.

"Yes, yes I did. But how soon it was over! How weak I felt afterwards, and then how homesick for my forest . . ." The tree's voice faded away.

Just then, a sharp wind blew the golden star right out of the little girl's hand, and made her shiver. And when Anna turned back to the little fir tree again, all its dry brown needles had fallen.

THE BOX

Ann Cameron

My mother was at a meeting. And my father had an errand to do.

"Will you kids be all right till I get back?" he asked.

"Yes," we said.

"Fine," my father said. "I may have a surprise for you."

"Great!" I said.

My dad left.

"I wonder what your surprise will be," Gloria said.

"Me too," Huey and I said, both at the same time.

The three of us stayed in the garden, taking turns swing-jumping. We didn't hear my dad coming back. It started getting dark and hard to see.

"I jumped farther than you," Huey said.

83

"You didn't," I said.

"Did too," Huey said.

"Did not, bean sprout," I said.

"Did not, WHAT?" my father said. He *had* come home. He was on the porch.

"Just *did not* was all I said."

"He called me 'bean sprout'!" Huey shouted.

"BEAN SPROUT!" my father roared. "He called you BEAN SPROUT?"

"I think I'll be going home now," Gloria said, very softly. She was already in the shadows, halfway out of the garden.

My father stepped out of the porch door. He put down a big cardboard box he was carrying.

"Wait a minute, Gloria," my father said. "I'd like you to stay. I have something in mind for these boys!"

84

I looked at Huey. "We can forget the surprise," I whispered.

"A surpise is coming," Huey whispered back. "But it won't be nice."

We all followed my father into the house.

"Are you going to send us to our room?" I asked.

"No," my father said. He had a scary smile.

"Are you going to make us wash windows?" Huey asked.

"No," my father said. He smiled again, like a tiger.

"What *are* you going to do?" Gloria asked.

"I have an idea about these boys, Gloria," my father said, just like he and Gloria were best friends. "I think they need to go through a potentially dangerous situation together. Then they may like each other more."

"What do you mean, a 'potentially dangerous situation'?" I said.

"I mean one that *could* be dangerous if you don't handle it right." My father smiled again, like a cobra.

"Like what?" Huey said.

"I know you boys like animals," my father said. "It wouldn't be anything much. Something like – live alligators. Maybe – sharks."

"Sharks!" Huey said. He reached for my hand.

"Now you boys make yourselves comfortable," my father said. "Gloria and I will be back in a minute."

The two of them walked outside to the porch. Gloria looked back at us. Her eyes said goodbye forever.

Huey and I sat on the couch.

"Is Gloria going to help carry in the sharks?" he asked.

"I don't know!" I said. "Huey, I'm sorry I called you 'bean sprout'."

"That's O.K.," Huey said.

"It's taking them a long time," I said.

We waited. Huey started rubbing his special laser ring that is supposed to fry your enemies to a crisp, although actually it couldn't even fry an egg.

Gloria and my father came back. They had the cardboard box my father had left on the porch.

"Hold it level, Gloria," my father said.

Inside the package something skittered.

"Not sharks," Huey whispered to me. "Maybe – live snakes!"

Gloria and my father set the box down in front of us. It was tied with strong cord. I moved my feet away from it.

"Now your job," my father said to us, "will be to open this box."

"Okay." Huey said, rubbing his ring.

"I don't want to," I said.

Gloria looked at me sympathetically. Even my father looked a little bit sorry.

"I don't want you to go into this without a fighting chance," he said. "Wait a minute."

He went into the kitchen.

I looked at the box. I tried to sense what was inside it. All I could sense was darkness. And breathing.

"Gloria," I whispered quickly, "do you know what's inside there? Would you say it's really dangerous?"

"I would say" – Gloria began – "that if I were you, I would say my prayers."

"Well, here you are," my father said cheerily.

He was carrying two kitchen knives.

I started making a plan. Huey and I could stab the box to shreds. Afterwards, we could find out what *had been* inside. I picked up one of the knives.

"Sorry," my father said. "The knives are for later. You have to open the box with your bare hands."

"With our bare hands?" Huey repeated. He didn't look so brave any more.

"Right!" my father said. "And be gentle. That's a good box. I may want to use it again."

"Couldn't this wait until tomorrow?" I said. Sometimes my father gets over his strange ideas in a day or so.

My father smiled his tiger-cobra smile. He raised his eyebrows.

"No," he said. "But I'll help you a little."

He took one of the knives and cut the cord on the box. That left only a little piece of tape on the top between whatever it was and us.

"Can't you tell us *anything* about what's in there?" I said.

"Just this," my father said. "They're hungry!"

Whatever it was, there was more than one!

"Come on, Julian," Huey said. He was rubbing his laser ring.

"Ready," I said.

We each took hold of one top flap of the box. We pulled in opposite directions so hard we fell on the floor. Nothing came out of the box at us.

We got up. We moved closer to the box.

"It's the surprise!" Huey said.

In one corner of the box were two baby rabbits. They blinked in the light. Their long ears trembled. One was brown. One was white.

Huey put his hand into the box. The white one smelled it.

"They're brothers," my father said, "and they're hungry."

Huey picked up the white one and held it in his hands.

I picked up the brown one.

"You said they were dangerous," I said.

"Could be," my father said. "If you boys don't take those knives and cut them some lettuce and carrots, they might start nibbling your shirts."

So we cut up lettuce and carrots while Gloria held the rabbits.

"Well, what about names?" my father said.

I thought of the toughest name for a rabbit I could. "Mine is Jake," I said.

"And what about you, Huey?" my father asked.

"Wait a minute. I have to think," Huey answered. He shut his eyes.

In a minute he opened them. He didn't say anything.

My father said, "Come on, Huey. What is it? Tell us."

A big grin spread across Huey's face.

"Bean sprout," he said.

THE
SILVER CUP

Joan Aiken

Joe's daily run for the newspaper took seven minutes. Two minutes up the sandy lane, one more to the paper shop and back, three talking to Mr Stubbs, one running home downhill.

Mr Stubbs, an old sailor, swept the village street with a broom and long-handled pan. "I like to be out every day talking to people," he said.

One morning Joe asked him about a pile of stones and sand in a plastic sack which had lain outside the post office for weeks.

"British Telecom folk left it," said Mr Stubbs. "I shan't touch it. Let 'em take it. Maybe if I shifted it, they'd turn me into a toad."

Another time, Joe asked about the two white-painted posts outside the Green Dragon pub, which had been knocked flat in the night.

"Maybe the Green Dragon did it," said Mr Stubbs.

91

A month before Christmas, Joe noticed a silvery metal cup wedged into the sandy bank at the corner where the lane met the village street.

"What do you think this is?" said Joe.

Mr Stubbs puffed out his white moustache thoughtfully.

Today was very cold. Frost silvered the grass like sugar on strawberries. Mr Stubbs had on his blue knitted cap. His nose was red as a strawberry.

"Tell you what," he said at last. "I think Santa Claus put that there for someone to make him a Christmas pudden."

"He did?" Joe was surprised. "Why?"

"He got no time to make his own, does he? Always driving round with those reindeer."

"But," said Joe, "Christmas only comes once a year."

"Ah? *Here* that's so. But what about in space?" said Mr Stubbs. "What about out there? It's always Christmas somewhere, out there. Old Sandy Claws is at it the whole year long, dashing from one star to another. And the planets. And the sun. All those moons. *He* don't get no three weeks' holiday."

"You think we ought to make him a Christmas pudding?" said Joe.

"I do," said Mr Stubbs.

"I'll ask Mum," said Joe.

Next day he told Mr Stubbs, "Mum says we can make a Christmas pudding if I can wash that cup really clean." He lifted the sandy metal cup out of

the tuft of grass where it had lodged. "Mind you, Dad says it's only a hub cap."

"Ah," said Mr Stubbs. "Off the sleigh, likely."

"Do sleighs have hub caps?"

"Those that run on ball-bearings do." Mr Stubbs sniffed the frosty air. "Going to be a white Christmas. The birds think so, and they know."

"Why?"

"Cousins of Sandy Claws, they be. All that

Claws family know about the weather. They know where it comes from. You can see 'em fly off the other way." He pointed. "See, the sky's all black in the north. And the birds is going south."

Joe took the silver cup home and rubbed and scrubbed and scraped it until his Mum said it was clean enough to put Christmas pudding mix in.

She had been beating up eggs and milk and flour and butter and rains and currants and candied peel and nutmeg and cinnamon and allspice and brandy; and, as well, she had dropped in a thin, worn, old, silver penny piece, more than a hundred years old, which had belonged to Joe's great-granny. "For luck," she said. "Whoever finds it in his helping gets a wish."

"Even if Santa Claus finds it?"

"Of course."

When they all stirred the gooey pudding mix it was spooned into three big bowls and also the metal cup that Joe had brought home. Wax paper was laid on top, and cloths tied over, and the puddings were boiled for hours.

"When will they be done?" Joe kept saying, and Mum kept saying, "Not yet. Christmas pudding has to be cooked for a really long time."

The smell in the house while the puddings were cooking was so dark and rich and strong that you could have eaten the air with a spoon.

Outside, the birds had gone quiet. It was growing colder and colder. Every morning Joe scattered crumbs. Birds would come with a swish and flutter. Every crumb would be gone before Joe was back in the kitchen.

Smoke went straight up from the chimney, like a line ruled to the middle of the sky. The ground was hard as brick.

"Soon it'll snow," said Mr Stubbs.

But it didn't; not yet.

The puddings were put away at the back of the pantry, with the little one in its silver cup.

At last came Christmas Eve. Joe and his dad walked to the woods and cut branches of holly and pine. They were stiff and rustly and smelt of magic. There was a sprig of mistletoe, with waxy white berries like pearls. And the Christmas tree was in a pot, ready to be hung with lights and shining balls. But that would not happen till Joe was in bed.

He hung up his stocking.

"Now can I leave Santa's pudding for him?" he asked.

"Wrap up warm and run fast, then," said Mum, "for it's colder than I've ever known."

Dad went with Joe. It was dark. They could feel the frost crunch under their boots. The air was full of bell-music; tingle-tangle, dingle-dangle, ding-dong, dong, dong.

"You'd think the air would break in splinters," said Joe, sniffing its iciness.

The silver cupful of Christmas pudding was hidden carefully in the middle of a tuft of frosty grass.

96

"Will he be able to find it?" said Joe.

"Certain to," said Dad. "Let's run all the way home."

Next morning there was still no snow.

After undoing his stocking, and after breakfast but before the presents on the tree were opened, Joe raced up the lane. There would be no newspaper, of course, on Christmas Day, but he wanted to see if Santa Claus had taken the pudding.

As Joe reached the village street, a few snowflakes began to fall. The sun, very low and red, had been trying to shine, but now it snuggled into a cloud, as it if had decided to go back to bed.

There was Mr Stubbs, with his broom.

"On Christmas Day?" said Joe, very surprised, but Mr Stubbs said, "People stay out late, Christmas Eve, and leave all kinds of rubbish. That's not nice for Christmas Day."

And he dropped two cans and a crisp bag into his pan.

Joe ran to the tussock where he and Dad had put the pudding, and found the cup was gone. There was a round dent where it had been.

He felt pleased, but also a little worried.

"It's gone," he said, "but how do we *know* that Santa took it? Perhaps those people who dropped the cans might have found it."

"Humph," said Mr Stubbs, tugging his moustache, staring at the sky. "That's true. How *do* we know? That's a hard one."

But then he said, "Hey – boy! Look at the sky!"

Joe looked at the sky. The sun was still nestled behind a round, dark cloud. And out of the cloud, and other scattered clouds, flakes of snow, black and busy as bees, were pouring down.

And round the cloud, all the way round, like a flaming, many-coloured collar, there ran a rainbow. A complete circle of rainbow, bright and glowing.

"Well, blow me!" said Mr Stubbs. "A whole, round rainbow. I never in all my life at sea saw *that!*"

The snow pelted down, whitening the ground,

and the rainbow hung, flashing, and the man and the boy stood staring at it. Gradually it faded, as the snow fell thicker and thicker.

"Well," said Mr Stubbs, "reckon that was from old Sandy Claws to say thank you for his pudden. Now I'm off home, for I can't sweep up all this snow. And you'd best get back to your presents."

So Joe raced home down the lane, holding the rainbow inside his mind, like a silver cup,

BABOUSHKA

Traditional Russian tale
retold by Nora Clarke

O nce upon a time, there was an old woman called Baboushka who lived all alone in a little house deep in the forest. She was always busy cooking, cleaning or sewing, and as she worked she would sing to herself. She sang old songs and new songs, and even songs she made up; for it could be lonely in the forest and Baboushka liked to keep herself cheerful. The main road was far away and there were few visitors to the little house, so she was very surprised one winter afternoon to hear loud noises coming towards her through the trees.

"Perhaps it's a bear!" she thought, and trembled. But no, a bear wouldn't crunch through the snow like that. She listened again. Tramp, tramp, tramp. She must have visitors! At once Baboushka ran into the house and put some more logs on the fire. She set the big, black kettle on the hob. A few minutes later, there was a loud knock on the door. Baboushka jumped.

"Who is it?" she called in a scared little voice.

"We are travellers," came the reply. "We are very tired and have lost our way. Can you help us?"

"Come in," cried Baboushka, and she flung open the door. "You are welcome to rest by my fire on this bitter day." A young man came in, smiling gratefully, and leading an older man. Then a third followed, shaking the thick snow from his coat. All three wore rich clothes, and the man who came last had shining gold rings in his ears.

While Baboushka busied herself heating a thick soup and cutting bread, the travellers told her they were journeying in search of a baby prince. "His star was guiding us," they explained, "but the sky is so full of snow that we can't see it any more."

"Don't worry," said Baboushka helpfully. "When you've eaten and rested, I'll show you where the road is, and then you won't need to follow a star!"

"You are very kind," answered the youngest man, "but only the star leads to the Christ child."

Baboushka was astonished. "A child and a star! What can this mean?"

The three men told her that the star was the sign of a holy child's birth and they showed her the rich presents they were taking to him. When she saw them, Baboushka's kind heart rejoiced.

"I wish I could see this child," she murmured.

"Come with us," they cried, "and help us in our search!"

But Baboushka shook her head sadly, thinking that she was much too old to travel, and began

ladling out the soup. And when the three men had eaten and rested, they thanked her and set off again through the trees.

The house seemed empty when they had gone, as Baboushka sat rocking slowly in her chair. "I would so like to see the baby prince," she whispered over and over again. Suddenly she jumped to her feet. "And I will! I'll join the search ... there's nothing to stop me. I'll go tomorrow, so I will!"

Quickly, Baboushka packed a small bundle of clothes, and then she collected together her greatest treasures to take to the holy child: a carved wooden horse, a little cloth ball, an old doll, a few painted fir cones and some pretty feathers she'd found in the forest.

Early the next morning, she wrapped up warmly and left her little house. She tried to find the path the travellers had taken, but fresh snow had covered their tracks.

"Have three kings passed this way?" she asked a farmer.

"Kings! In this weather? What a foolish question," roared the farmer, and he stomped away crossly. Then she met a shepherd.

"Have you seen a bright star?" she asked him eagerly.

"Thousands, old woman," he chuckled. "Right above you. And they all shine brightly!"

A herdsman trudged past with his herd of cattle.

"Have any baby princes been born here lately?" Baboushka questioned him anxiously.

"We've plenty of babies," he replied, "but not a prince among them."

She tramped on wearily, stopping everyone she met to ask, "Have you seen the Christ-child, please?" but no one could help her.

And to this very day, Baboushka has never stopped searching; she still travels her country looking for the baby prince. And whenever she meets with a child who is sick or unhappy, she digs deep into her pack and always finds a little toy to make them smile.

BRER RABBIT'S CHRISTMAS

Joel Chandler Harris
retold by Nora Clarke

Once upon a bright clear winter morning Brer Fox stole into Brer Rabbit's garden and dug up a big sackful of his best carrots. Brer Rabbit didn't see him as he was visiting his friend Brer Bear at the time. When he got home he was mighty angry to see his empty carrot-patch.

"Brer Fox! That's who's been here," cried Brer Rabbit, and his whiskers twitched furiously. "Here are his paw marks and some hairs from his tail. All my best winter carrots gone! I'll make him give them back or my name's not Brer Rabbit."

He went along, lippity lip, clippity clip, and as he went along his little nose wrinkled at the fragrant smell of soup coming from Brer Fox's house.

"Now see here," he called crossly. "I just know it's my carrots you're cooking. I want them back so you'd better open your door."

"Too bad," chuckled Brer Fox. "I'm not opening my door until winter is over. I have plenty of carrots thanks to my kind friend Brer Rabbit, and a stack of other food for Christmas as well. I'm keeping my windows shut and my door bolted, so do go away. I want to enjoy my first bowl of carrot soup in peace."

At this, Brer Rabbit kicked the door, blim blam. He hammered on the door, bangety bang. It wasn't any use. My, he was in a rage as he turned away. Kind friend Brer Rabbit indeed! He stomped off, muttering furiously. But soon he grew thoughtful, then he gave a hop or two followed by a little dance. By the time he reached home he was in a mighty good temper. Brer Rabbit had a plan all

worked out. He'd get his carrots back and annoy Brer Fox into the bargain!

On Christmas Eve, Brer Rabbit heaved a sack of stones on his shoulder and climbed up onto Brer Fox's roof. He clattered round the chimney making plenty of noise.

"Who's there?" Brer Fox called. "Go away at once. I'm cooking my supper."

"It's Father Christmas," replied Brer Rabbit in a gruff voice. "I've brought a sack full of presents for Brer Fox."

"Oh, that's different," said Brer Fox quickly. "You're most welcome. Come right along down the chimney."

"I can't. I'm stuck," Brer Rabbit said in his gruff Father Christmas voice. Brer Fox unbolted his door and went outside to take a look. Certainly he could see somebody on the roof so he rushed back inside

and called,

"Well, Father Christmas, don't trouble to come down the chimney yourself. Just drop the sack of presents and I'll surely catch it."

"Can't. That's stuck too," yelled Brer Rabbit and he smiled to himself. "You'll have to climb up inside your chimney, Brer Fox, then catch hold of the piece of string around the sack and you can haul it down yourself."

"That's easy," Brer Fox cried, "here I come," and he disappeared up the chimney.

Like lightning, Brer Rabbit was off that roof and in through the open doorway. There were his carrots in a sack, and on the table was a fine cooked goose and a huge Christmas pudding. He grabbed them both, stuffed them into the sack and he ran. Chickle, chuckle, how he did run.

That old Brer Fox struggled up the chimney, higher and higher. He couldn't see any string but he felt it hanging down so he gave a big tug. The sack opened and out tumbled all the stones, clatter bang, bim bam, right on Brer Fox's head. My, my, he certainly went down that chimney quickly. Poor Brer Fox! He'd lost his Christmas dinner and the carrots, and now he had a sore head.

That rascally Brer Rabbit laughed and laughed but he made sure he kept out of Brer Fox's way all that Christmas Day and for some time afterwards.

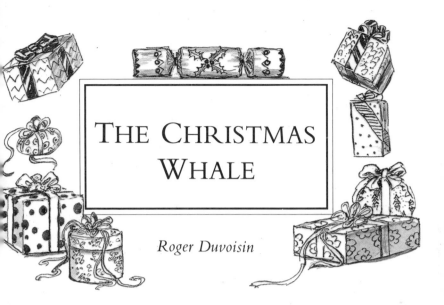

THE CHRISTMAS WHALE

Roger Duvoisin

What a blustering, freezing, nipping wind blew at the North Pole that year! Snowdrifts piled so high around Santa's igloo that the red chimney, sticking out, looked like a red cherry on the top of a cream pie. Santa had to dig a tunnel to come out of the house; and each day he had to make the tunnel longer, for the snow would not stop falling.

"I daresay it's worse than the blizzard of eighty-eight," said Santa, coming out of the tunnel one day.

Small wonder that in such weather Blitzen the reindeer suddenly felt a chill run down his back and had to be put to bed with aspirin, hot tea, and a hot-water bottle.

Small wonder that Vixen, in the middle of a game of solitaire . . .

Then Comet as he was practising on the flute . . .

And then all of Santa's reindeer, one after the other, felt the chill down their backs and had to be put to bed with aspirin, hot tea, and hot-water bottles. It was a flu epidemic.

"Curse the snow and the wind and the cold and the flu!" cried Santa. "They *would* do that to my reindeer just before Christmas!" And Santa sat at his desk to telephone to his doctor: "Get your dog sleigh ready and come over at once. It's urgent!"

When the doctor came in, Santa trotted behind him from bed to bed, looking very worried.

"Well, nothing very grave," said the doctor after taking the last reindeer's temperature. "Two or three weeks in bed and everything will be all right."

"All right?" exclaimed Santa, wringing his hands in despair. "All right, with Christmas only a week away! But that's a catastrophe! What shall I do? Who will draw my sleigh? That's a catastrophe!"

112

"A catastrophe," repeated Santa when the doctor had left. "That's what it is – a catastrophe." And he brooded so much that Mrs Santa called him four times for lunch before he even heard.

"Now, don't despair, and eat your soup before it's cold," said Mrs Santa. "You still have eight long days to find a way out of your troubles."

"Eight days," Santa lamented after dinner. "That's a real catastrophe.

"By all the chimneys! By all the stockings! By all the Christmas trees in all the world! That's a *catastrophic* catastrophe!"

While Santa thus lamented and walked back and forth in his igloo with no idea coming to him, all his friends, the North Pole animals, talked of nothing but the flu epidemic and the coming Christmas.

"Poor old Santa," they said to one another. "Imagine his missing the first Christmas in five hundred years! And with all these toys and gifts piled up in the big shed! Couldn't we find a way to help him?"

"Ah," said the huskies, "if we could only fly, wouldn't we draw Santa's sleigh through the skies! But we can't, alas."

"Ah," said the white bears, "if we could swim like the porpoises, we would make a boat out of the sleigh and draw it through the waves. But we can't, alas."

"Ah," said the walruses and the seals, "if we could gallop fast like the wind we would sweep the sleigh round the world. But we can't, alas."

"And us gulls," said the gulls, "if we were as strong as albatrosses, *we* would draw the sleigh. but we aren't, alas."

"Well," said the cod (he was full of good fish sense), "fine intentions won't help Santa. What he needs is one idea with no ifs in it. And, mind you, I have one."

The cod called Santa, who was still walking back and forth by himself, now in his igloo, now at the edge of the ice, and said: "Stop walking and muttering for a moment and listen to me, Santa, and your worries will swim away like frightened sardines. What you want is something fast enough, strong enough, to carry your packages round the world. I have that thing for you – the whale! Her back is as broad as an iceberg, she is as strong as the waves in a storm, and she is as fast as the wind. Go and ask her."

"My little cod," said Santa, "I think that you are the cleverest fish in all the seas. I am going to see the whale right now."

The whale was playing far away among the grey waves, and Santa whistled and tramped and shouted almost until dinnertime before she noticed him. Then she came at once, splashing the icy water around her. She got Santa all wet.

She was indeed kind and obliging. "I am ready. When do I start?" she said simply when she heard what Santa wanted.

The very next day Santa rubbed his hands with joy while the walruses, the seals, the white bears, and the gulls came to fetch the mountain of Christmas packages which stood in the big shed.

One by one the packages were carried away to the water's edge to be piled into a new mountain on the broad back of the kindly whale.

So many boxes were brought up that the kindly whale stood lower and lower in the water.

"Watch my water line," she warned. "Don't let me sink below it. I've got to breathe, you know." She was so frightened that she would not let Santa put a last little box of building blocks on the top of the mountain. It was all safely tied up with Christmas ribbons.

"We'll take it next year," said Santa.

While the white bears, the walruses, the seals, the

gulls, and Mrs Santa cheered, Santa and the kindly
whale departed.

Santa was so happy that he whistled "Jingle
Bells" almost all the way to New York, which
was the first stop.

Upon their arrival in New York a pilot climbed
upon the head of the kindly whale to lead her into
the harbour toward two little tugboats, which
waited to push her gently to the pier.

The pier soon looked like an ant nest, with little
men running to and fro, carrying packages on their
backs, while the customs officers watched with

indulgent smiles and never opened as much as one package for inspection.

From New York, Santa and the kindly whale went to South America, and to Africa and to Europe, and to Australia.

And then, very weary, but very happy, they went back home to the North Pole, knowing that in spite of the flu, gift giving would go on that Christmas just as it had for the past years.

The icy cold water of the North never felt so deliciously refreshing to the kindly whale, just as the odour of the hot leek soup which Mrs Santa had prepared for Santa never seemed more appetizing to him.

"Really," he said to Mrs Santa as she helped him put on his warm slippers, "I found whale travelling extremely convenient. If there were not so many pictures and stories about my reindeer and me, I would ask the kindly whale more often. After all, on Christmas cards, I would look just as glorious riding a whale as I do driving my sleigh. Whales are very decorative."

THE CHRISTMAS ROAST

Margaret Rettich
translated by Elizabeth D. Crawford

Once a man found a goose on the beach. The November storms had been raging several days before. She had probably swum too far out, been caught, and then tossed back to land again by the waves. No one in the area had geese. She was a real white domestic goose.

The man stuck her under his jacket and took her home to his wife. "Here's our Christmas roast."

They had never kept an animal and had no coop. The man built a little shed out of posts, boards and roofing board right next to the house wall. The woman put sacks in it and put an old sweater on top of them. In the corner they put a pot with water in it.

"Do you know what geese eat?" she asked.

"No idea," said the man.

They tried potatoes and bread, but the goose

120

wouldn't touch anything. She didn't want any rice either, and she didn't want the rest of their Sunday cake.

"She's homesick for the other geese," said the woman.

The goose didn't resist when they carried her into the kitchen. She sat quietly under the table. The man and the woman squatted before her, trying to cheer her up.

"But we aren't geese," said the man. He sat on a chair and tried to find some band music on the radio. The woman sat beside him, her knitting needles going clickety-clack. It was very cosy. Suddenly the goose ate some rolled oats and a little cake.

"She's settling down, our lovely Christmas roast," said the man. By next morning the goose was waddling all over the place. She stuck her neck

through the open doors, nibbled on the curtains, and made a little spot on the doormat.

The house in which the man and woman lived was a simple one. There was no indoor plumbing, only a pump. When the man pumped a bucket full of water, as he did every morning before going to work, the goose came along, climbed into the bucket and bathed. The water spilled over, and the man had to pump again.

In the garden there was a little wooden house, which was the toilet. When the woman went to it, the goose ran behind her and pressed inside with her. Later she went with the woman to the baker and then to the dairy store.

When the man came home from work on his bicycle that afternoon, the woman and the goose were standing at the garden gate.

"Now she likes potatoes, too," reported the woman.

"Wonderful," said the man and stroked the goose on the head. "Then by Christmas she will be round and fat."

The shed was never used, for the goose stayed in the warm kitchen every night. She ate and ate. Sometimes the woman set her on the scales, and each time she was heavier.

When the man and the woman sat with the goose in the evening, they both imagined the most marvellous Christmas food.

"Roast goose and red cabbage. They go well together," said the woman and stroked the goose on her lap.

The man would rather have had sauerkraut than red cabbage, but for him the most important thing was the dumplings. "They must be as big as my head and all the same size," he said.

"And made with raw potatoes," added his wife.

"No, with cooked ones," asserted the man.

Then they agreed that half the dumplings should be made with raw potatoes and half with cooked ones. When they went to bed, the goose lay at the foot and warmed them.

All at once it was Christmas.

The wife decorated a small tree. The husband biked to the shop and bought everything they would need for the great feast. He also bought a kilo of extra-fine rolled oats.

"Even if it's her last," he said with a sigh, "she should at least know that it's Christmas."

"I've been wondering," began the woman, "how, do you think, should we... I mean... we still have to..." But she couldn't get any further.

The man didn't say anything for a while. "I  can't do it," he said finally.

"I can't either," said the woman. "I could, if it were just any old goose. But not this one. No, I can't do it, no matter what."

The man grabbed the goose and fastened her on to his baggage carrier. Then he rode his bicycle to a neighbour's. In the meantime, the woman cooked red cabbage and made the dumplings, one just as big as the next.

The neighbour lived far away, to be sure, but still not so far that it was a day's journey. Nevertheless, the man did not come home until evening. The goose sat contentedly behind him.

"I never saw our neighbour. We just rode around," he said ashamedly.

"It doesn't matter," said the woman cheerfully. "While you were gone, I thought it over and decided that adding something else to the dinner would just spoil the good taste of the red cabbage and the dumplings."

The woman was right, and they had a good meal. At their feet the goose feasted on the extra-fine rolled oats. Later all three sat together on the sofa in the living room and enjoyed the candlelight.

The next year, for a change, the woman cooked sauerkraut to go with the dumplings. The year afterwards there were broad noodles to go with the sauerkraut. They were such good things that nothing else was needed to go with them.

And so time passed. Goose grew very old.

M any years ago, a hunter from the Northlands trapped a great white bear. It was such a fine bear that he decided to present it to the king of his country. So the man and the bear set out even though it was winter and the snow was falling thick and fast. They tramped and tramped, but the king's palace was far away and it began to grow dark. The hunter was cold and weary. Suddenly, through the trees, he glimpsed a little cottage with lights a-shining.

"I'll ask for shelter for the night," he told the big white bear as he knocked on the door. It was opened by a tall thin man with a very worried face.

"Please may we come in? We are both very tired with trudging through the snow," said the hunter.

"Oh no, no," replied the man, whose name was Halvor.

"We are going to see the king, this fine bear and I. We only want to warm ourselves at your fire for the night."

"Impossible! You can't stay here." Halvor waved his arms about. "I'm sorry, I can't help you."

The bear gave a sad little grunt, while the hunter shivered and stared at Halvor in surprise. He tried again.

"We don't need much room and we won't disturb you. Please don't turn us away into the snow." But Halvor shook his head.

"I'm not an unkind man," he said. "I'd like to help you, but it's Christmas Eve, a time of great trouble for me."
He opened the door wider.

"Look at my wife and my three children hurrying to get things ready for Christmas. See how sad and worried they look," Halvor went on. "They never enjoy Christmas because year after year the trolls come. Many, many trolls. They chase us out, throw our food about, then break all the dishes. They tear down the decorations, they scream, they shout. Oh no, Christmas is not a happy time for us."

"Trolls!" exclaimed the hunter. "Trolls don't frighten us. Please let us into your warm house. Trolls won't bother us, will they, Bear?"

At last Halvor let them both in and they slept in a warm corner near the stove. Halvor's wife had prepared a delicious dinner and on Christmas day she put everything on the table, which the children decorated with holly and candles. All of a sudden, quicker than a flash, the trolls appeared. They came down the chimney, in at the windows, under the door and even up through the floorboards. Some were tall and some were small. Some had long noses and no tails; some had long tails and long ears. All of them were very, very ugly. Halvor and his family grabbed their warmest clothes and ran and locked themselves in the woodshed.

Then those trolls attacked. They bellowed. They screamed. They threw the turkey and vegetables about and smashed the dishes. They squashed jellies into the floor and blew bubbles in the milk. They jumped on the table and paddled in the custard. Some smaller trolls emptied jars of jam and rubbed it over the windows. The noise was terrible but the man and his bear watched quietly by the stove. At last, when there was nothing left to damage, the naughtiest troll of all saw the big bear

lying peacefully in the corner. He grabbed a sausage, pushed it on a fork and waved it right under the bear's nose.

"Pussy, pussy, have a sausage," he shouted in a silly voice. The bear sniffed. It was a good smell. At once the troll pulled the sausage away, out of the bear's reach.

"Pussy, pussy, here you are." Again the troll waved the sausage in front of the bear and again he snatched it away. Slowly the bear lumbered to his feet. He opened his mouth wider and wider. He let out a great roar, then another even louder one. He chased those trolls up the chimney, out of the windows and under the floorboards, from the smallest to the largest, until there was not one left.

"You are a fine bear," the hunter said proudly. "Here, have a sausage or two." So the bear ate the sausages; then he licked some jam from the windows because bears love sweet things.

"You can come out of the woodshed now," the hunter shouted. "My bear has chased away all the trolls."

Halvor, his wife and three children crept back to the cottage. They could hardly believe the trolls had gone, but when they saw it was true they set about cleaning up the mess with a will. There was enough food for a good supper before they all went to bed, and the next day the hunter and the bear went on their way to the king. Halvor never saw them again.

A year later, on Christmas Eve, Halvor was chopping wood in the forest when he heard someone calling his name. "Halvor! Halvor!"

"Yes, I'm Halvor. What do you want?" he replied.

"Is that big white cat still living with you?" It was a troll's voice.

"She certainly is," shouted Halvor. "And she has seven kittens now, each one bigger and fiercer than the last. Do you want to visit her?"

"No! We'll never come to your house again," the trolls screamed. And they never did. Ever afterwards Halvor, his wife and their three children enjoyed their Christmas Day in peace and contentment.

THE FAIRY SHIP

Alison Uttley

Little Tom was the son of a sailor. He lived in a small white-washed cottage in Cornwall, on the rocky cliffs looking over the sea. From his bedroom window he could watch the great waves with their curling plumes of white foam, and count the seagulls as they circled in the blue sky. Tom's father was somewhere out on that great stretch of ocean, and all Tom's thoughts were there, following him, wishing for him to come home. Every day he ran down the narrow path to the small rocky bay, and sat there waiting for the ship to return.

December brought wild winds that swept the coast. Little Tom was kept indoors, for the gales would have blown him away like a gull's feather if he had gone to the rocky pathway. He was deeply disappointed that he couldn't keep watch in his favourite place. A letter had come, saying that his father was on his way home and any time he might arrive. Tom feared he wouldn't be there to see him, and he stood by the window for hours watching the sky and the wild tossing sea.

"What shall I have for Christmas, Mother?" he asked one day. "Will Father Christmas remember to bring me something?"

"Perhaps he will, if our ship comes home in time," smiled his mother, and then she sighed and looked out at the wintry scene.

"Will he come in a sleigh with eight reindeer pulling it?" persisted Tom.

"Maybe he will," said his mother, but she

wasn't thinking what she was saying. Tom knew at once, and he pulled her skirt.

"Father Christmas won't come in a sleigh, because there isn't any snow here. Besides, it is too rocky, and the reindeer would slip. I think he'll come in a ship, a grand ship with blue sails and a gold mast."

Tom's mother suddenly laughed aloud.

"Of course he will, little Tom. Father Christmas

comes in a sleigh drawn by a team of reindeer to the children of towns and villages, but to the children of the sea he sails in a ship with all the presents tucked away in the hold."

She took her little son up in her arms and kissed him, but he struggled away and went back to the window.

Christmas morning came, and it was a day of surprising sunshine and calm. The seas danced into the cove in sparkling waves, and fluttered their flags of white foam, and tossed their treasures of seaweed and shells on the narrow beach.

Tom's mother's face was happy and excited, as if she had a secret. Her eyes shone with joy, and she seemed to dance round the room in excitement, but she said nothing.

Tom ate his breakfast quietly – a bantam egg and some honey for a special treat. Then he ran outside, to the gate, and down the slippery grassy path which led to the sea.

"Where are you going, Tom?" called his mother. "You wait here, and you'll see something."

"No, Mother. I'm going to look for the ship, the little Christmas ship," he answered, and away he trotted.

The water was deep blue, like the sky, and purple shadows hovered over it, as the waves gently rocked the cormorants fishing there. The little boy leaned back in his sheltered spot, and the sound of the water made him drowsy. The sweet air lulled him and his head began to droop.

Then he saw a sight so beautiful he had to rub his eyes to get the sleep out of them. The wintry sun made a pathway on the water, flickering with points of light on the crests of the waves, and down this golden lane came a tiny ship that seemed no larger than a toy. She moved swiftly through the water, making for the cove, and Tom cried out with joy and clapped his hands as she approached.

The wind filled the blue satin sails, and the sunbeams caught the mast of gold. On deck was a company of sailors dressed in white, and they were making music of some kind, for shrill squeaks and whistles and pipings came through the air. Tom leaned forward to watch them, and as the ship came nearer he could see that the little sailors were playing flutes, tootling a hornpipe, then whistling a carol.

He stared very hard at their pointed faces, and little pink ears. They were not sailor-men at all, but a crew of white mice! There were four-and-twenty of them — yes, twenty-four white mice with gold rings round their snowy necks, and gold rings in their ears!

The little ship sailed into the cove, through the barriers of sharp rocks, and the white mice hurried backward and forward, hauling at the silken ropes, casting the gold anchor, crying with high voices as the ship came to port close to the rock where Tom sat waiting and watching.

Out came the Captain — and would you believe it? He was a Duck, with a cocked hat and a blue jacket trimmed with gold braid. Tom knew at once he was Captain Duck because under his wing he carried a brass telescope, and by his side was a tiny sword.

"Quack! Quack!" said the Captain, saluting Tom, and Tom of course stood up and saluted back.

"The ship's cargo is ready, Sir," said the Duck. "We have sailed across the sea to wish you a merry Christmas. Quick! Quick!" he said, turning to the ship, and the four-and-twenty white mice scurried down to the cabin and dived into the hold.

Then up on deck they came, staggering under their burdens, dragging small bales of provisions, little oaken casks, baskets, sacks and hampers. They brought their packages ashore and laid them on the smooth sand near Tom's feet.

There were almonds and raisins, bursting from silken sacks. There were sugar-plums and goodies, pouring out of wicker baskets. There was a host of tiny toys, drums and marbles, tops and balls, pearly shells, and a flying kite, a singing bird and a musical-box.

When the last toy had been safely carried from the ship the white mice scampered back. They weighed anchor, singing "Yo-heave-ho!" and they ran up the rigging. The Captain cried

"Quack! Quack!" and he stood on the ship's bridge. Before Tom could say "Thank you," the little golden ship began to sail away, with flags flying, and the blue satin sails tugging at the silken cords. The four-and-twenty white mice waved their sailor hats to Tom, and the Captain looked at him through his spy-glass.

Away went the ship, swift as the wind, a glittering speck on the waves. Tom waited till he could see her no more, and then he stooped over his presents. He tasted the almonds and raisins, he sucked the goodies, he beat the drum, and tinkled the musical-box and the iron triangle. He was so busy playing that he did not hear soft footsteps behind him.

Suddenly he was lifted up in a pair of strong arms and pressed against a thick blue coat, and two bright eyes were smiling at him.

"Well, Thomas, my son! Here I am! You didn't expect me, now did you? A Happy Christmas,

Tom, boy. I crept down soft as a snail, and you never heard a tinkle of me, did you?"

"Oh, Father!" Tom flung his arms round his father's neck and kissed him many times. "Oh, Father. I knew you were coming. Look! They've been, they came just before you, in the ship."

"Who, Tom? Who's been? I caught you fast asleep. Come along home and see what Father Christmas has brought you. He came along o' me, in my ship, you know. He gave me some presents for you."

"He's been here already, just now, in a little gold ship, Father," cried Tom, stammering with excitement. "He's just sailed away. He was a Duck,

Captain Duck, and there were four-and-twenty white mice with him. He left me all these toys. Lots of toys and things."

Tom struggled to the ground, and pointed to the sand, but where the treasure of the fairy ship had been stored there was only a heap of pretty shells and seaweed and striped pebbles.

"They's all gone," he cried, choking back a sob, but his father laughed and carried him off, pick-a-back, up the narrow footpath.

On the table in the kitchen lay such a medley of presents that Tom opened his eyes wider than ever. There were almonds and raisins, and goodies in little coloured sacks, and a musical-box with a picture of a ship on its round lid. There was a drum with scarlet edges, and a book and a pearly shell from a far island, and a kite of thin paper from China, and a love-bird in a cage. Best of all there was a little model of his father's ship, which his father had carved for Tom.

"Why, these are like the toys from the fairy ship," cried Tom. "Those were little ones, like fairy toys, and these are big, real ones."

"Then it must have been a dream-ship," said his mother. "You must tell us all about it."

So little Tom told the tale of the ship with blue satin sails and gold mast, and he told of the four-and-twenty white mice with gold rings round their necks, and the Captain Duck, who said "Quack! Quack!"

When Tom had finished, his father said, "I'll sing you a song of that fairy-ship, our Tom. Then you'll never forget what you saw."

There was a ship a-sailing,
A-sailing on the sea.
And it was deeply laden,
With pretty things for me.

There were raisins in the cabin,
And almonds in the hold,
The sails were made of satin,
And the mast it was of gold

The four-and-twenty sailors
That stood between the decks
Were four-and-twenty white mice
With rings about their necks.

The Captain was a Duck, a Duck,
With a jacket on his back,
And when this fairy-ship set sail,
The Captain he said "Quack".

It was such a lovely song that Tom hummed it all that happy Christmas Day, and it just fitted into the tune on his musical-box. He sang it to his children when they were little, long years later, and you can sing it too if you like!

EARLY ON CHRISTMAS MORNING

Lois Lamplugh

Two days before Christmas Mrs Venn sat by the fire and wrapped up family presents. Tacker worked at a model Tiger Moth on a sheet of newspaper spread out on the brown chenille tablecloth.

"There, there's Granfer's," Mrs Venn said with satisfaction, adding a small parcel of tobacco and hand-knitted socks to the pile beside her. "I want for you to go over and give him that, Tacker, early Christmas morning."

"Me?" Tacker looked round in alarm. "You coming too?"

"No need for me to come, is there?"

"You always have."

"Well, yes, but I reckon you're old enough now to take your grandfather his presents without me being there."

"I won't know what to say."

"What to say? Bless me, boy, say 'Merry Christmas'. You don't need for to make a speech. You're not scared of Granfer all of a sudden, are you?"

And so, two mornings later, in the cockcrow dark, with only a slice of bread and butter and a cup of tea inside him, Tacker set off for his grandfather's cottage. It was a morning of black frost under a cloudy sky, and daylight came slowly. From most cottage windows he passed, lamplight or candle-light shone out, some upstairs, some down. He was surprised when he reached his grandfather's cottage to see that *his* light was still upstairs, since his grandfather was usually up early.

Tacker called "Granfer?"

"Tacker? Come up then, I'm still in bed."

The boy groped his way up the short, steep flight of stairs, opened the door of his grandfather's room and advanced uncertainly to the bedside. "Merry Christmas this is for you," he said in one breath, and put the package on the counterpane.

"Merry Christmas," the old man said. He was smoking his

first pipe of the day. He took it out of his mouth and propped it in the tray of the flowery china candlestick beside him while he picked up the package and turned it over in his hands.

"What's this, eh? Present? Your Mam send you? That's it, then. Now, seeing I'm a bit slow this morning, will you do something for me?" He handed Tacker a box of matches. "Go down and put a light to the oil stove, and set the kettle on for me tea, will you?"

Tacker went carefully down the stairs and along to the tiny kitchen.

Outside the closed door he stopped in surprise. Under the latch was a small hole, and yellow light showed through. Who had lighted the kitchen lamp, if his grandfather had not been down? It could not have burned all night – it would have run out of oil. He listened. No sound. Was someone there? He was fearful and yet curious, and he longed to run upstairs again. But that would look daft.

Cautiously he raised the latch and peered into the room. The lamp burned on the table; there was no one there, but propped against the table stood a bicycle. Completely bewildered, he gazed at it. *A bicycle*, in Granfer's kitchen? He didn't ride a bicycle. Or at least he hadn't for a long time – not since the night he tumbled off into the stream before the wall was built alongside the village street. Tacker could remember hearing about that; he had been about four at the time. But what had happened to Granfer's bike after that he did not know.

This one was not new, but it gleamed with a fresh coat of yellow enamel, picked out with white. The handlebars and wheel rims shone bright; the tyres looked unused. There was no pump or lamp. Pinned to the saddle was a piece of paper.

He went forward and read the message on it.

"For Tacker. Happy Christmas from Granfer."

A bicycle. *Now*. He did not need to wait until his birthday, after all.

He crouched down, examining it. It had been beautifully cared for, oiled and greased and kept free from rust, even before it was repainted. But his grandfather always took care of things; he liked to tell of the way he had cared for his fine stallions when he walked them as a younger man. The churchyard, tended by him, was well weeded and full of flowers, and he scythed the grass close, even on such forgotten graves as John Hobson's.

Tacker stood up and took hold of the hand-grips, and bounced the front wheel on its deep-patterned tyres. His, his, his. He could ride out, down the street, all round the village like the others did (and as he had done before now, but only on borrowed bikes); round and round, swooping and whooping. He turned, ready to wheel it out, but remembered. He hadn't even said thank you.

The door opened and his grandfather came in. He had put on trousers and the fisherman's jersey he wore for gardening.

"Well, will it do?" he asked.

Tacker did a thing he had not done for a long time. He flung his arms round his grandfather and hugged him. He said "Thank 'ee, Granfer, thank 'ee," over and over again.

I'm sorry I couldn't manage to put on a pump, and a lamp," said his grandfather.

"That don't matter," Tacker said, thinking that the lamp, at least, mattered a good deal; as he couldn't ride after dark without it, that meant that at this time of year he wouldn't be able to go out after four o'clock.

"You've done it up handsome," he said. "Is it the bike that – is it the one you used to ride?"

The old man nodded. "That's the one. It was a wet night, and dark and slippy, and I came off in the stream. Didn't hurt the bike much, but it shook me bones. Wet to the skin, I was, and cold, so I got rheumatiz. Just didn't ever want to ride it again, after that."

He saw Tacker to the gate. "You can ride that thing, I suppose?"

Tacker swung a leg over the saddle to show him.

"Um. Beats me how you all learn it. Well, straight home, mind. Don't go gallivanting off."

Tacker only smiled by way of answer, and waved as he let the cycle carry him away downhill until he was out of sight. Go straight home on his first ride on his own bicycle? Of course not. He must have one circuit of the village, at least.

He stood up out of the saddle and rushed full tilt down the hill below the forge; then pedalled hard up the opposite slope, and just reached the top without dismounting. Sharp right along the north ridge, past cob walls, stone walls, hedges, and then round the corner by the dipping place and so home.

Elated, hungry, and breathless, he ran into the indoor warmth.

His mother came out of the kitchen and smiled broadly at sight of him.

"You managed that errand for me, did you?" she asked.

He hugged her, too. "It's lovely, the bike. I never guessed. Have you seen it, all done up? Come and look."

"Ah that'll do later. Breakfast's keeping warm on the range. Come in and we'll have our presents before anything else."

When it was Tacker's turn to be given his parcels, he opened the two from his parents first. In one was a bicycle pump; in the other, a lamp.

ROOM FOR
A LITTLE ONE

Maggie Pearson

A winter's night. Starlight. Frost-bright. The coldest night of the year.

The travellers at the inn, though, they were snug and warm. So many travellers! (Where did they all come from?) Making work enough for six. But there was only one of Jenny and a little one, at that.

"Clear those dishes, Jenny!"

"Pour the wine!"

"Fetch water from the well!"

"Make up the fire! There's no more wood. Jenny, you'll have to fetch some more."

Off went Jenny, wrapping an old blanket round her against the cold, leading the donkey to carry the wood.

Back they came again, the donkey nothing but a pile of wood on legs. Nothing to be seen of Jenny

under the blanket but her little bare feet, blue with cold.

The donkey's stable was no more than a bit of tattered thatch leaning up against the wall, with just room inside for a little one.

But somehow they made it room for two, so Jenny could warm her feet against the donkey's warm coat before she went back to work.

In the yard, a poor old ox stood all alone in the cold.

"Come into the stable," said Jenny. " We can make room for a little one."

And they did – for the ox and the donkey, too.

Back she went to the kitchen, to serving at table

and washing the dishes and sweeping the floors and mending the fires.

And here were two more weary travellers knocking at the door. A man and a lady.

"No room!" said the landlord. "No room!" No room.

"Come with me," whispered Jenny. "Come into the stable. We can make room for a little one."

And they did. Room for the man and the lady, the ox and the donkey, too.

Upstairs in the inn the travellers were sleeping four, five, six to a bed.

Downstairs they dozed on benches and tables and draped themselves over the banister-rail.

Jenny worked on till everything was spick and span. Then, though she was ready to fall asleep right there where she stood, she fetched bread and wine, fried up a few small fishes and took them over to the stables.

"Come in, Jenny!"

"There's no room."

"There's room for a little one."

And there was. Room for the man and the lady, the ox and the donkey, for Jenny, too – and for one more. A new-born baby, lying in the manger.

Jenny knelt down and gave the baby her finger to hold.

She didn't feel cold or tired any more. She felt like dancing. Outside the frost sparkled and danced. The tired old world felt young again.

Through the tattered thatch, Jenny could see that the stars were dancing too.

Somewhere there was music, singing:

He has come!
He is here!
Christ is born!

Over field and furrow the message ran, waking the rabbits in their burrows, the birds in the trees and the sheep high up on the hills.

The shepherds heard it and came hurrying down.

And three weary travellers – kings, no less – who had followed a bright star mile after mile . . .

"May we come in?"

"Is there room for us?"

"Room for me?"

"Room for a little one?"

And there was room – room for every one.